Men of Stone

Men of Stone

by Gayle Friesen

Kids Can Press

Published in Canada by
Kids Can Press Ltd.
29 Birch Avenue
Toronto, ON M4V 1E2

Published in the U.S. by
Kids Can Press Ltd.
4500 Witmer Estates
Niagara Falls, NY 14305-1386

Edited by Charis Wahl
Cover designed by Marie Bartholomew
Interior designed by Stacie Bowes
Printed and bound in Canada

CM 00 0 9 8 7 6 5 4 3 2 1
CM PA 00 0 9 8 7 6 5 4 3 2

Canadian Cataloguing in Publication Data

Friesen, Gayle
    Men of Stone

ISBN 1-55074-781-9 (bound)   ISBN 1-55074-782-7 (pbk.)

I. Title

PS8561.R4956M46 2000   jC813'.54   C00-930013-9
PZ7.F74Me 2000

For my parents, Peter and
Martha Neumann, with love

ACKNOWLEDGMENTS

Thank you, Alison and Christy, for the many, many readings. Thank you, Charis, particularly for clarity this time. I'd also like to thank David Giesbrecht at CBC for giving me the Mennonite "thumbs up."

Many people served as inspirations for this book. My aunts and uncles — especially David Neumann and Margarete Huebert — who carry the stories of Russia with them, and the Mennonite traditions deeper still.

And also Nick — for dancing.

1

The lines on her face were like earth that had gone too long without rain. It was a face that told a story, but not one I wanted to hear. She was a hundred years old if she was a day.

"Aunt Frieda would like to come for a visit" was the way Mom had opened the family conference a week ago.

"Aunt who?" my sisters and I asked simultaneously.

"You know," Mom insisted.

No we didn't.

"Your father's aunt ... your great-aunt," Mom prodded. "She's asked if she could come and spend some time with us."

"Why?" Again, the question was more or less unanimous. Unusual too, since we hardly ever agreed on anything.

Mom shrugged and poured another cup of coffee. Her chin had twitched the way it did when something was bugging her. "She said she was old."

"That's her reason?" I asked.

"I guess so, I really don't know her that well. I haven't even seen her since the um, funeral."

The um-funeral. My dad. He died ten years ago. I was five.

"It's not the best time for me, between marking papers and working on my thesis, but I didn't know how to say no. It will only be for a few weeks."

"A few weeks?" Joni said it, but we were all thinking it. "It's hard enough to get anything done around here as it is. Where'll she stay in this matchbox?"

"I thought the den," Mom answered almost timidly. Joni scared her, I think. Hell, she scared all of us.

"The den?" Joni shrieked. If there had been birds in the trees, they were flying south after that. "That's where I paint."

"It's where I rehearse," Mad, the aspiring actress added.

Beth was calmer, but determined. "Mom, I have exams coming up too — pastries and dainties in less than a week! Dad had a ton of relatives. Can't she visit them?"

"Apparently she wants to visit us. You girls are not making this easy. I'm sorry if you're not happy with it, but I've told her she's welcome. Your father would have wanted me to do this." Mom drained her coffee like it was a shot of whiskey and left the room.

The girls kept on grumbling, but no one asked my opinion. It was accepted that I had no opinions.

This was okay because, after fifteen years, I'd figured a few things out. For most of my life I'd known I didn't quite fit. But one day on the Discovery Channel there was a show about a tribe of Amazons. This mythical tribe was completely female — no guys allowed. All male children were either exiled to live with their fathers or killed. It made sense to me, considering my household.

Anyway, now Mom and this Aunt Frieda person were standing in our kitchen.

She was about five foot nothing with snowy white hair under a plastic rain kerchief, which she untied and tucked away in neat folds inside her purse. She shook each girl's hand formally and repeated each of their names. She stood straight, looked right into their eyes.

"And you're Ben! Of course you are."

She gave me a big hug. I looked over her head — she only came up to my chest. My sisters' mouths were hanging open, and they were speechless. I was thinking that anything that made my sisters speechless couldn't be a bad thing, when she let go as suddenly as she'd taken hold.

I laughed nervously. "Hi, er, Aunt … uh," I said finally.

She took one of my hands and covered it with hers. I was trapped.

"I've been looking forward to meeting you for a very long time."

"I, uh, thanks," I said, feeling my ears go red.

"*Nah yo*," she said, looking around the kitchen, taking us all in with her keen brown eyes. "Thank you for letting me come. I promise not to get in the way."

"Not at all, Frieda. It's nice to have you," Mom offered, a polite lie.

"Well, now, I know it's a little odd … my coming here and all, but one day I woke up and thought to myself, Frieda, you're not getting any younger. It's time to stretch these old legs while they still work!"

Mom smiled an uneasy smile. "Of course."

"And I wanted to get to know Neil's family. He was my favorite nephew … Maybe I shouldn't say that, but he was such a wonderful man. I still have the postcards he used to send me — painted those pretty pictures himself!" She smiled around the room. If she'd been a comedian, she'd have tapped the microphone and said, Is this thing on?

We hardly ever talked about our dad. Only Joni would occasionally refer to him as "our father who art in heaven." And here was this old lady throwing his name around like loose change.

"Why don't I show you where you'll be staying," Mom finally said. She picked up the luggage and they left.

"Well," said Beth.

"Huh," said Mad.

"Lucky us. We have ourselves our own personal Mary Poppins," Joni said, and clomped up the stairs to her room. My sister wears army boots.

Beth elbowed me in the stomach. "You should have seen your face when she hugged you, Benny."

"I thought you were going to pass out," said Mad.

"Poor Benny," they chimed together, like the identical twins they are.

I went to my room, closing the door behind me. Nobody would barge in. It was an unspoken rule.

I sat down on my bed and wondered what I'd done to deserve one more female relative. It already felt like a boarding school for girls around here.

When I was little I'd wanted to go to that school. Dress me up? Sure. Put me in one of Mad's backyard plays? Why not? My last official performance was in Mad's production of *Peter Pan*. You'd think my being a boy might have given me a shot at Peter Pan, but that role went to Mad. Beth was Wendy, of course. How about Michael? John? Nope, both parts went to Joni. And me? I was Tinkerbell! Enough to seriously screw with my precarious male psyche.

Eventually I figured out that I was different — I think around the time Mad chased me through the house trying to get me to wear a dress because, "How else can we play *Little Women* if you're not Amy?" Then I knew it was a question of survival. If

I didn't want to spend the rest of my life in a dress, I had to run for it.

It became really obvious around puberty — mine, not theirs. Theirs was cause for celebration throughout the land, with Mom congratulating them on "becoming women." But when my voice started to crack and my hormones showed up, you'd have thought it just occurred to them that I wasn't a girl. What I remember about the one talk Mom tried to have with me wasn't the words, just the different shades of color that traveled over her face. When she got to "nocturnal emissions," it was like watching a sunset. By the time she broke out in a sweat, handed me a book and left the room, I figured I had a couple of months, tops, to live. Thank goodness for books is all I can say.

Mom took me fishing once. Just the two of us. We rented a rowboat and all the equipment up at Salmon Lake. We spent most of the morning untangling line and trying to put poles and reels together. I was eight — what did I know? By the time we got everything out on the water and managed to get the motor running — someone from the bait shop had to help us — the fish were down at the bottom of the lake to avoid the midday heat. I don't think I even got a nibble, but the thing is, I had a great day, a really great day. We ate our sandwiches and drank iced tea straight from the thermos. We didn't have to talk or anything … just sat there. I dove into the water when it got too hot and said maybe this was something we could do every weekend. She nodded, but she didn't say yes and her eyes were sad.

2

"Hey, Ugly, wait up," Fish called as I was about to cross the street to school. I had left home early for volleyball tryouts.

"Hey, Fish ... whew, what's that smell? You still sleeping with your hamster?"

"Dad's after-shave," he said, rubbing his broad chin, underlining the fact that he shaved regularly while I had as much need to shave as an orange.

"And we all know how important personal hygiene is to you, you big macho stud."

He grinned. "As much as this mixed volleyball thing sucks, you have to look for the opportunities."

"Yeah, I know. Melody Schneider." I checked my watch. "Two point two seconds into a conversation and you haven't even said her name yet. True love fading?"

"Shut up." He grinned again, showing off even white teeth, the smile known to attract any girl within eyeshot. The smile that had set his parents back at least three thousand bucks. "I saw Kat checking you out at volleyball the other day, so don't go all monk on me." He grabbed me in a halfhearted headlock. If it had been wholehearted, I'd be dead.

I shook him off. "The only thing she's ever said to me was that I was out of position. She doesn't even know my name."

"Small detail." He shrugged.

"Right." I opened the heavy door to the gym. Fish bulldozed ahead of me. I followed him to the locker room where we stowed our stuff. Stan was already there, doing the laces up on his Queen Mary sneakers.

"What's that smell?" he asked, sniffing as Fish opened the locker beside him.

"Success," Fish answered.

Stan nodded. "I heard Melody's sick today," he said, with no trace of emotion, but I knew he was lying even without the wink he gave me.

Fish sent up a howl before charging into the gym to see for himself.

Stan watched him go, shaking his head. "He's such a putz."

I laughed, but more at Stan than Fish. His last recorded smile was in Grade 5, and his deadpan face always made me laugh.

"How's Great-Auntie? She came yesterday, right?"

I crammed my bag into a locker. "Late."

"So you haven't been through the cheek-pinching, my-how-you've-grown, come-here-and-give-me-a-hug routine yet?" He was still tying his laces methodically.

"I don't think she's the cheek-pinching type," I said, brushing over the fact that everything else he'd said was dead on.

Stan finally finished tying his shoes and stood, towering above me like a giraffe on steroids.

"Coming?" He half turned. "Your lady awaits." Stan always talked like that, like dialogue out of those dusty old books he was always reading.

I kept my face toward the locker so he couldn't see it turn red. "In a sec," I answered, and he left.

I'd been so careful not to tell those jerks how I really felt about Kat. I had the worst luck with girls, which was like this huge irony considering I was surrounded by them at home. All those years of being used for kissing practice, and I knew more about makeup and feminine hygiene products than any male on the planet — none of it counted for anything.

The first girl I liked was Janice Helger — Grade 7. All year I just stared, working up the courage to talk to her. She had this nose that flipped up at the end, and it totally bowled me over. I actually had dreams about it. In art, all the girls I drew had the same nose. I was obsessed. Finally one day I walked up to her at recess and said, "I like your nose," and I made this little gesture with my finger, this little flipping gesture on my own nose.

Later that day I got hauled into the principal's office for a big lecture on ... I don't know, respect or something. Mr. Jefferson gave me a detention, and for the rest of the year the girls treated me like gum under a desk.

In Grade 8, I went to a new school and I figured, like an idiot, I'd try again. But not with Janice Helger, who hates me to this day.

Alicia Nadeau. She had long black hair and skin the color of caramel. But I didn't say a thing about any of that because I'd learned my lesson. I was wise now. Instead, I used all the listening skills I'd picked up at home, and Alicia and I actually had a few conversations after math class. One day she asked me to have lunch with her. It was a nice spring day and I was pretty happy, thinking I was making great progress. We were sitting there outside — me chewing my burger — when she started to talk about her hips, and the warning bells went off.

"I hate my hips," she said. "All the women in our family have them ... they're so wide and gross. I hate them."

Then she looked at me, and I knew this was my cue. I took my time, I swallowed my burger and tried to recall everything I'd learned. Finally, I was sure.

"But hips are like, natural, right?"

I swear this was ALL I said. End of picnic.

That's when I gave up on women. It was as if they spoke another language. I might be able to speak "sister," but "girl" was another thing entirely.

Fish stuck his head through the open doorway. "Ben, you coming?"

I slammed my locker door and followed him into the gym.

"Hey, hey — it's Ballerina Boy!" Claude shouted from across the cavernous room.

I ignored him and crossed over to Stan and Fish. But the clod didn't stop.

"How about a nice pirouette or a *pas de deux?*" Claude yelled.

I figured it wouldn't help my case much to shout back that a *pas de deux* was actually a dance involving two people.

"Want me to, um, talk to him?" asked Fish, his meaty fists clenched by his side.

"Leave it," I said, volleying a ball over to Stan.

"It's not like you still do that stuff," he said in a low voice, as if the stuff I used to do was run drugs for the mafia.

I quit dance just after I came to this school, but my past still haunted me. The sad truth is that I really am a pretty good dancer.

Claude was in a particularly bulldog mood today. He crossed the floor with a couple of his goon-squad buddies.

"I need some culture today, Miss Ben Conrad. Pretty please ... just a little spin around the floor?"

"Why don't you just piss off?" Fish growled menacingly.

"Ooh. Ballerina Boy has a bodyguard," Claude said, and his two sidekicks laughed at his wit.

Before I could say anything, Stan had stepped up.

He wasn't as meaty as Fish, but he was tall, and with his non-smile policy he could look pretty intimidating. He moved within an arm's length of Claude's smirky face and stood there for at least ten seconds without saying a word.

Claude was starting to look uncomfortable when Stan spoke softly. "I think you're aware that my friend Fish has a short fuse." He gave it the long pause. "My suggestion would be to move your sorry butt out of here."

Claude backed up a step, forcing a smile onto his face. "Later, Ballerina Boy." And he walked away, flanked by the goons.

Fish laughed and tried to high-five Stan, but Stan's hands remained at his sides. He isn't big on touching. "That guy watches too many gangster movies," Stan said. Then he tossed a ball into the air as if nothing had happened.

I'd spent six years at Miss Fleur's Academy of Dance, learning tap, jazz and, yes, even ballet. My sisters went, and I, being young, thought all that jumping would be more fun than sitting in a corner waiting for them to finish while my mom had her head stuck in a book, so I asked if I could join. I had to ask more than once. Finally my mom said that if I was really sure, I could give it a try.

Here's one more interesting fact. All three of my sisters are as graceful as a traveling troupe of left-footed bears. Joni danced the way she painted — full of fury. For Mad it was just another role that she played, and not one she particularly liked. And Beth treated it like a recipe — one part this, one part that and a teaspoon of salt. But it was different for me. I was the one with the talent. Another gruesome bit of trivia — I actually enjoyed it. When I went to my first class it felt right, familiar. Like the inside of me could finally stretch all the way out.

The kids at elementary school didn't seem to care one way or the other. It wasn't a big deal. By Grade 7, it was about to pay off — there I was, one of two boys in the whole dance school, surrounded by girls. Pay dirt was around the corner.

But when I started high school, someone caught wind of my dirty little secret, and suddenly I was Ballerina Boy. All those stupid jokes and whispers. One particularly witty kid said he was going to go as me on Halloween, dressed in a tutu. That finally got to me, so I quit. My sisters were disappointed, but I think my mom was relieved. We never talked about it.

As I bumped the ball back to Stan, I caught sight of Kat, lost IQ points and completely forgot that I'd given up on women. That happened whenever I saw her. It wasn't as if she was the most beautiful girl in the world, or even the school. Probably Melody was prettier, like one of those girls in a magazine with everything in the right place.

Kat had this kind of angular thing going on with her blunt, shoulder-length hair and sharp features ... long, lean torso and really great legs. She was good at track, fast and smooth. And — this sounds stupid, but — she always seemed really clean. She just shone. The whites of her eyes were so white they were almost bluish and so clear you felt you could just walk inside them and it would feel like a sunny day. I'd only talked to her once. I lasted four seconds before elastic bands inside me were popping and fraying.

Mostly I watched her from far away. That's why I wanted to be on the volleyball team. I just wanted to be in the same room with her. How pathetic was that?

The coach called us to form teams. I walked to the middle of the floor and took a position. Kat was on Claude's team. Just on the other side of the net I could see the muscles on her face tighten as she got ready. And I got to thinking about what it would feel like to touch the side of her face. I wondered if the muscles would relax and how her skin would feel ...

Then, crash, right in my jaw. A meteor shower burst in my head, and I went down on my knees.

"Ever hear of calling 'service'?" Fish yelled, as I struggled to my feet, holding my jaw.

"Maybe Conrad could try watching the ball instead of Kat's T-shirt?" Claude yelled back.

As I straightened up, I saw Kat's already flushed face brighten to the shade of Mad's favorite lipstick. She stood totally still for a second and then walked off the court.

As she passed, I tried to explain, "I wasn't ... uh, er, ... I ..." My throat tightened as though a noose had been pulled.

"Guys are pigs," she hissed, yanked the girls' locker room door open and disappeared inside.

"Somebody just shoot me," I muttered to Stan.

"I'd say, for all intents and purposes, buddy, you're already dead."

Claude and his laugh-track friends howled on the other side. The coach yelled for us to play ball. Fish turned around and grinned. "Look at the bright side, Ben. She knows your name now!"

I leaned forward with my arms outstretched, waiting for another serve, but all I could see was Kat's embarrassed face, and it made me feel like a slug.

3

Stan was waiting for me outside the school gates at the end of the day with an unlit cigarette hanging from his lip.

"Where's Fish?" I asked.

Stan cupped his hands and lit up. "Who knows? Probably with his lady fair."

I nodded and followed him. "He's got it bad."

"It's going around," he said, offering a rare half smile.

"I think I pretty much blew any chance I might have had today," I said.

"You know what they say — the course of true love never did run smooth," Stan said, taking a long drag.

"Well then, I'm in excellent shape," I said, climbing into his beat-up truck. "Shepherd asked me why you weren't in history today."

"What'd you tell him?"

"I said you were probably out in the quad smoking." I grinned.

"That's helpful." Stan gunned the engine, leaving a stream of black exhaust in his wake. "You take any notes?"

"Yeah," I answered. "They're right here ... color coded and double spaced ... somewhere ... Now where did I put them?" I pretended to look through my knapsack, which was empty except for an old lunch bag that smelled like seventh-grade tuna fish.

Stan and I weren't exactly on target to make the honor roll.

His truck made conversation difficult, so when he pulled up at my house, I just yelled, "See ya!" and he drove off.

It startled me when I walked through into the kitchen to see an old lady sitting at the table. I had forgotten she was here.

"Oh, uh, hi," I said, knocking over a chair with a loud bang.

She jumped, and as I scrambled to right the chair, I hoped I hadn't given her a heart attack. She looked so tiny and shriveled — like an apple that had been left in the sun too long.

"It's me — Ben," I said loudly.

She winced slightly and managed a small smile. "They say my hearing is good for an old lady."

"Oh, right. Sorry," I muttered quietly, growing red.

I stood there like an idiot, not knowing what to do or say. It was like meeting a long-lost relative who lived on ... Mars. What do you say to a Martian?

"Would you like some tea?" she asked, getting up slowly.

I waved her to sit down. "I'll get a cup," I offered.

She sat down again. "My legs work pretty well too. They're the last to go."

I smiled a little. I handed a mug over, and she filled it with dark black tea. I hate tea, but I took the cup and added a couple of tablespoons of sugar and lots of milk.

"Where's everybody?" I asked, still standing and holding the cup awkwardly.

"Sit down," she ordered, sounding like a tiny general. "Your sisters aren't home yet and your mother's gone to her university ... the library, I think she said. Imagine a grown woman still in school!"

"Part-time. She teaches the rest of the time," I said. "She's working on her master's, uh, in administration, Aunt Frieda." I tried out the name for the first time.

"Well, good for her," she said. Her eyes were warm and shimmery, tucked in behind a map of wrinkles. "*Ach*, Ben, you've gotten so big."

I shrugged. The last time she'd seen me I would have been five. I wondered if she was going to pinch my cheek. But her hands were folded in front of her.

"I used to be bigger," she said.

I drained the tea in one final gulp, burning my throat in the process. "I've got lots of homework,"

I said truthfully. What I didn't say was that I had no intention of doing it.

"Yes, your mother was telling me that you've been having some trouble with your schoolwork."

"I'll bet she was," I muttered. Better grades were my mother's answer to everything. Not that she ever seemed to wonder what the question was.

"She seems worried about you," Aunt Frieda continued.

Okay, now I was getting twitchy. This was moving into none-of-her-business territory. What did she think she knew about me, anyway?

"She wants me to get into a good university," I tossed back, checking out the doorway. Just four big steps and I'd be out of the room.

"And what do you want?" she asked, looking into my eyes unflinchingly.

I almost answered, I don't know what the hell I want, but the door opened and Joni and Beth poured in. They came to a dead halt when they saw us, as if they'd also forgotten she was here.

"Oh, hi," Beth said.

Joni just stood there, wearing her regular all-black ensemble and half snarl.

Physically, all my sisters took after my mom, and when they were little, people mistook them for triplets. That stopped when the girls discovered hair dye, though. Mad changed her color and style for every new part that came her way. Beth mostly stuck to her original blond ... with occasional highlights when she was feeling adventurous. For Joni, bluish black was the most consistent choice. She rarely let her light roots show and the effect was ... sobering.

"Hello, girls. How was your day?"

I leaned back in my chair and watched the scrutiny shift.

"Good, pretty good, thanks." Beth sat down beside me. She and Mad had graduated last year, and now Beth was at some cooking school.

Joni mumbled something about homework, which was a joke since she hadn't cracked the spine of a book since junior high. How she was going to graduate this year, even from the alternative program, was one of life's big mysteries. "It's not relevant" was her usual battle cry. Personally, I appreciated her stand, as it helped diffuse some of Mom's pressure on me. Now Joni just pulled a juice box out of the fridge and left the room.

"She's an artist," I said to Aunt Frieda, by way of explanation.

"Like your father," she said.

Not really. Dad painted landscapes and people with actual faces ... recognizable things. But I didn't say anything. Mostly I was thinking how weird it was to have someone here who had no clue how abnormal a family we were.

"Would you like some tea?" Aunt Frieda asked Beth.

Beth shook her head. "I really should get supper started," she said.

"I could help," Aunt Frieda offered.

Beth's smile froze. The kitchen was her territory, and nobody ever dared intrude. Not that anyone really wanted to.

"That's okay ... you're our guest," Beth answered.

"Now, now ... none of that. We're all family. I don't want any special favors. Just give me a job." She waited, and I smiled at the quiet stubbornness on her face.

"Um, well, I suppose you could ... uh ... chop the zucchini for me," Beth said, shooting a "help me" look across the room. I shook my head ever so slightly, and Beth's eyes narrowed.

I knew I'd probably be shot for insubordination, but I was enjoying the way my sisters' perfectly organized world was crumbling. Take it from someone who's been bossed around his whole natural-born life — this was an event.

Girls ruled here. Period. It would be fun to see this hundred-year-old woman shake things up. For now, though, I got up to leave.

"Tell Joni I need her for something," Beth called out to me.

"Uh-huh," I said, still smiling at the look on Beth's face.

Taking the stairs two at a time, I paused at the top. The upper floor was the land of the Amazon women, and I hardly ever visited. I'd learned, soon after my tenth birthday, that this was where they walked around in their underwear. Wastepaper baskets were filled with wrappers and tissues that told me more than I wanted to know about the female body, and multicolored strappy things hung in the bathroom. I remember using one of their bras as a slingshot once — with the underwire ones you can get great distance — but nobody appreciated my ingenuity. Mostly I stayed away.

I stood outside Joni's door. The sign was up. DO NOT DISTURB. Underneath was scrawled in scarlet ink, *Already Disturbed*.

I knocked anyway, but softly.

"What?" she called out.

I took this as an invitation and stepped inside the dumpster she called a room. Directly across from me, above her bed, was her masterpiece to date, a huge mural painted on her wall. It was mostly dark shapes and vigorous crimson squiggles. She called it *Cramps*.

"Beth wants you," I said, turning to leave.

"Close the door," she ordered. I did. "She still down there?"

"No, she went back to Saskatchewan. She said you scared her."

Joni didn't even crack a smile. "She's so old," she said.

"Yeah."

"How old do you think she is?"

"Really old," I said.

"Yeah." Joni reached under her bed and pulled out a pack of cigarettes. She lit one.

"Mom's gonna love the smell of cigarette smoke in the house."

She waved the smoke out of her face and opened a window. "I'm stressed, okay?"

"So, this is more stressful for you than the rest of us?" I dared to ask.

She gave me a long, Joni glare. "I feel things that the rest of you are afraid to feel," she answered, blowing smoke into the backyard.

There was no place to sit without moving a pile of laundry, so I stood beside her chest of drawers. It was littered with beauty products, mostly for hair. I picked up a long slender cylinder and read the back instructions.

"This one says, 'Do not smoke until hair is dry.' Doesn't that make you nervous at all?"

"Very funny."

"Well, it is, kind of — using a beauty product that could, like, explode into flames. Wouldn't that ruin the whole effect?" I tried to keep a straight face.

"You guys have it so easy," she said, shifting to face me.

Here it comes.

"You can put a T-shirt and jeans on, swipe a comb somewhere in the vicinity of your head and you're ready to go out —"

"I know, I know." Why had I started this? I looked around the room for something white to wave. I surrender.

"And as far as self-immolation is concerned —"

"Huh? Self-immo ... what?"

"Lighting yourself on fire."

"Were we talking about that?"

She ignored my question. "Women all over the world have resorted to self-immolation as a way to protest how unfairly women are treated."

"That's, uh, horrible," I admitted, wondering how we'd gone from Aunt Frieda and hair spray to burning women. But at the same time not really wondering.

"You men rule the world," she said with finality and another long exhalation of smoke. I was being dismissed.

I exited quietly, closing the door behind me. Rule the world. Funny, you'd think that was the kind of thing I'd have noticed. I was lucky if I got to use the bathroom before noon.

I went downstairs and peeked into the kitchen. Aunt Frieda was sitting at the table peeling and chopping zucchini. Beth was at the sink. I tip-toed past the open door and made it to my room unnoticed.

I didn't come out again until I heard Mom enter the kitchen.

"Smells good," I said, sniffing deeply. "What is it?"

"Greek phyllo vegetarian pizza with seasonal greens," Beth answered. Ever since she'd started cooking school, she talked like a menu.

Stan and Fish would have scoffed, saying that unless meat was present, and large bloody chunks of it, it wasn't a meal. But in this house you ate what you were served. And, to be fair, Stan would have eaten it too, because he was madly in love with Beth. But afterward he would have raced directly to the nearest burger joint.

"Where is, uh, she?" I said carefully. The teapot and cup were gone, leaving no trace of her.

"In her room, reading," Mom answered. "Did you have a chance to chat with her?"

"Oh, sure. After school we chatted ..."

Mom looked suspicious. "She'll take a while to adjust, I guess."

I nodded, stuffing down one of Beth's biscuits, hot from the oven. It would take more than a few weeks to adjust to us.

"Try some of the papaya spread," Beth insisted.

"No thanks," I said with my mouth full. Even I had my limits.

Suddenly the door flew open, and I knew without looking that Mad had arrived. Madeleine — Mad — the younger (by twenty minutes) of the twins, never came into a room. She made an entrance. She was wearing her secondhand black cashmere cape draped around her shoulders. As she closed the door behind her, she pulled the cape off, flinging it across a nearby chair so the red satin lining provided a perfect throne for her to perch upon.

"It's unbearably cold out there," she breathed into her hands. "Unbearably." Then, "What's for supper, Beth?" This was said in her regular voice.

"Greek phyllo vegetarian pizza with seasonal greens," Beth answered.

"Sounds heavenly. Guess what, everyone?" Mad paused meaningfully. (All her pauses were meaningful.) "I think I have a shot at the commercial!"

There was a squeal of excitement from Beth. I managed to contain mine. Mad's been trying out for plays, commercials, movies — you name it — ever since I can remember. Sometimes she even snagged a part.

"Excellent! What's the part?" Mom asked.

"It's only a commercial, but it would be a foot in the door."

She should be a centipede for all the feet she's had in doors over the years.

"What's the part?" I asked, moderately curious.

"Well, let me set it up for you. It's the dead of winter. It's cold …"

"Unbearably cold?" I guessed.

She frowned, shaking her head slightly. "Everyone's ill … colds, influenza … strep throat. Oh! It's set in a pharmacy. I'd be, 'hacking cough desperately in need of relief.'" She stood and her cape slid to the floor in a crumpled heap. "I walk — stumble, really — into the store and make my way to the prescription counter." She gave an agonizing bark, her face contorting with pain. "'Please,' I say, 'don't you have something to relieve my scratchy throat?'" She added another meaningful pause and then bent to the floor to retrieve her cape. When she straightened, her voice was back to normal. "I think I really have a crack at it. You should have heard the other actors, with their pitiful 'ahems.' I think I really impressed the casting director."

"I'm sure you did," said Beth loyally. "I almost wanted to give you a spoonful of cough syrup right now!"

"How much money would you get for it?" Mom asked. She didn't like to talk much about our finances, but I knew she worried.

Mad shrugged. "I'm not sure." She tore open a biscuit and dumped the papaya goop on. "Mm, good stuff, Beth."

"Thanks. When do you find out about —"

"Next week, I —"

"You'll definitely get —"

"Thanks."

That's the way they spoke, as if they were on the same frequency most of the time. I think it made Joni — Miss I-feel-things — jealous sometimes, but I figured it was just a twin thing.

"What's up?" Joni asked, coming into the room wearing her paint-flecked overalls.

Mad reenacted her drugstore scene, only this time she laid it on even thicker.

"That's great, Mad." Joni smiled.

I paid attention. Joni rarely smiled. Mad caught it too.

"But?" Mad waited, head tilted forward.

"But nothing." Joni shrugged.

Mad shook her head. "You've got that look on your face."

"It's just that, well ..." Joni leaned back on the heels of her boots. "Wouldn't you feel you were selling out?"

I thought I heard Mom sigh, and then she left the room.

Mad's shoulders stiffened, and her head poked out from her neck like a turtle's. "What do you mean?"

"Well ... a commercial? It's not exactly Shakespeare, is it?"

I could hear Mad's quick intake of breath and Beth's backup gasp. The gauntlet had been thrown down. This could get interesting.

"Besides," Joni continued. "The whole point of coughing is that it's a sign that something is wrong, so cough suppressants are really dangerous ... as if they're disguising the truth. Philosophically, I'm opposed ..."

She was entering what I called the blah-blah-blah stage, and I could see Mad begin to boil. I settled back to see what would happen next. As dramatic as Mad could be, she needed a script —

words weren't always her best friends. I figured it came from having a twin who always finished her sentences. Mostly she just changed inflections, turning everything into a big performance.

"Can't you ever be positive about one thing, Joni? Does *everything* have to be ... I don't know, *have* to be ..."

She was way behind on verbal artistry. But she might do better in the technical scoring. I liked to judge these fights the way adjudicators scored my dance performances. Mad tended to be stronger in the screaming and hitting department — what I called the technical portion. Joni usually excelled in the artistic category — strong on verbal assault.

"Fight, fight, fight," I chanted under my breath.

Oops — tactical error on my part. Now they had a common enemy.

"Shut up!" they both bellowed.

"You guys ... cool it," Beth said quietly. If I was the judge, she was the referee.

That's when I noticed Aunt Frieda standing in the doorway. I wondered how much she'd heard. I thought maybe she'd bawl us out or something, but she smiled and walked to the middle of the room. The little munchkin just looked at each of us, then she came and stood beside me.

"Now this reminds me of Russia, when I was growing up," she said, and sat herself down at the table.

Mom came back into the room just then, so I couldn't ask her what she meant. But it sort of intrigued me. What could our house and all its weirdness have in common with her life?

As Beth pulled the pizza from the oven, I grabbed a couple of pieces and headed for the TV to watch my dinnertime shows.

"Not tonight, Ben," Mom called me back. "I want us to have a family dinner."

Family dinner? I stopped in my tracks. Since when?

I returned to the table.

Aunt Frieda didn't talk much during dinner. Mostly the girls and Mom talked around her. I think the phyllo pizza mystified her a little, and she only nibbled at it, like a rabbit at the edge of the garden.

"Ben," Beth said suddenly. "Did you make the team? I ran into Stan on my way home."

I shrugged. "We find out tomorrow, but I doubt it. Most of the —"

"Hey! Attitude, Benjo. You gotta have faith," she said, before I could finish.

"That's right, a positive mental attitude —" said Mad.

"— is what you need to succeed —"

"— in this world."

I lost track of who was saying what. I really missed my dinner-in-front-of-the-TV routine.

"Anyone who dances like you, Benny, could do

any sport you wanted. Although why you gave up dance —" said Mad.

"I'll never know," finished Beth.

"He was so good, Aunt Frieda. Even when he was a little guy. Remember that *Arabian Nights* piece, Beth? That girl — what was her name?" said Mad.

"Kelly Robertson?" supplied Beth.

"Yeah, Kelly Robertson. She injured her foot right in the middle of their duo and had to leave the stage. Ben didn't even blink, just finished on his own —"

"Even improvised some stuff. He was in his own world!"

"The crowd went crazy ... standing ovation. How old were you?" asked Mad.

I grunted and slid lower in my chair.

"Nine," Mad decided. "Only nine years old."

Then a small, reedy voice joined in, and somehow I heard it above the brass band.

"So then, why did you stop?" Aunt Frieda asked.

The room went quiet and even Joni looked up from her plate for the first time.

"I just, uh —"

"He quit," Joni said, taking her plate over to the sink.

"There's nothing wrong with quitting something that you've outgrown," Mom added, probably trying to be supportive.

"I didn't say there was anything wrong with it. Sometimes it's just too much. You give up. Stuff happens ... people die or leave and ... that's just the way it is," Joni said over her shoulder.

"We were talking about Ben's dancing." Mad looked perplexed.

"Joni, really," Mom interjected, rubbing her left eye. "Can't we have just one simple dinner?"

"Absolutely. Be my guest," she said, leaving the room.

Mom looked embarrassed and asked Aunt Frieda if she'd like to have a cup of tea. Aunt Frieda nodded.

It didn't take long for Beth and Mad to fill the kitchen with noise again, but fortunately the conversation stayed away from dance. For that, I was grateful to Joni. I didn't think anybody else really understood Joni, but I did, even when I didn't want to. She'd been the one with all the questions after the funeral.

"Why is he in that box?"

"Where is he now?"

"Why isn't he coming home?"

Horrible questions. But more horrible still was the silence afterward. As unprepared as we were for our dad to die, we were just as unprepared to discover that our mother didn't control the universe.

My dad colored the world with his paint-brushes. He was fun and loud, and there was always a fleck of yellow or blue in his hair. He smelled like paint thinner.

My mom held us together. She was the frame, narrow and solid, around our edges. None of us, especially me, expected her to fall apart. And except for that one day, she hadn't.

4

Stan showed up the next morning before school. He did this about once a week, to remain low-key about his crush on my sister. But the truth was, the nearest he came to a smile was when he saw her. He made me swear not to say a word to Beth, but I suspected she knew and kind of enjoyed it. Normally she wouldn't look twice at a "younger man" but Stan had taken kindergarten twice, so he was sixteen and had his license.

"Hey, Stanley, how's it going?" Beth chirped from behind the morning paper.

Beth was the only person on the planet allowed to call him Stanley.

His lips went perilously close to being upturned. "What smells so good?"

"Scrambled-egg wraps made with hand-pressed tortilla shells and a mildly spiced salsa," she answered happily. "Want some?"

I knew his head was hoping for bacon and eggs, but his heart answered. "Sounds fantastic."

"We're gonna be late," I grunted.

"Relax," he hissed, and I could see the back of his

neck turn red. In the interest of my own safety, I said nothing.

"No prob. It's a breakfast designed for a guy on the go," answered Beth, efficiently rolling the wrap in tinfoil, fluffing out the top end artistically.

Stan took a man-size bite and I could tell from the sudden look of pain on his face that a chunk of foil had hit a filling. But he recovered quickly. "Delicious," he said, looking directly into Beth's eyes.

"Good. I'm presenting in brunch class tomorrow."

"A-plus," Stan said, as I pushed him toward the door. "Thanks."

"What is your big hurry?" he growled once we were outside.

"A-plus?" I mocked him.

"Can I help it if your sister is an angel?"

I made a gagging noise, covering my mouth with my hand.

He ignored me and ate the wrap solemnly, the last lingering reminder of my sister.

"What do you think my chances are of making the team?" I asked.

Stan used his full mouth as an excuse not to answer. But the look on his face said it all.

Sure enough, when we checked out the list posted beside the gym doors, my name wasn't on it.

"It's a short season," Stan said, by way of consolation.

He went to his locker and I went to mine, picking up the pace as I walked. Who cared anyway? I knew I hadn't given it everything during the tryouts. I hadn't given anything everything since ... for a long time.

Fish was waiting at my locker. The look on his face said either his dog had been run over by a semi or he'd heard about the team.

"Man, that sucks," he said, punching me on the shoulder. I hid my wince as his steel knuckles made contact. "I was pulling for you."

"No big deal," I said, rubbing my shoulder once he'd turned to his own locker.

"It was pretty competitive ... so many guys tried out. Besides, if they weren't including girls this year, you'd have made it for sure. I mean, they had to include a certain number of girls so —"

"Yeah, yeah, yeah." I didn't want him pretending I was good at volleyball. I knew how it felt to be good at something. Sometimes I wanted to go back to it — dancing. But then I'd remember all the razzing and it just didn't seem worth it. Like Joni said the other day, sometimes it's too much and you just give up.

To make my day a complete write-off even before the bell, Claude appeared behind me.

"I'm so disappointed you didn't make the team, Ballerina Boy."

Fish slammed his locker shut and faced Claude, but I shifted myself between them. "Let's go, Fish," I said.

"Maybe you could make the cheerleading squad. You've got the moves," Claude called after us.

I saw Fish's entire body tense up. "Just say the word."

I kept walking, shaking my head so Fish had no choice but to follow. I knew he wouldn't attack without my say-so. I also knew he was wondering why I didn't take care of Claude myself.

"What's his problem with you anyway?" Fish finally grumbled once we were out of earshot.

"I dunno. His sister went to the same dance academy as me, so he's seen a few shows. Maybe ..." I trailed off.

"You didn't really like that ... stuff, did you?"

I didn't answer right away. "My sisters all went, so ..."

Fish looked heartened. "Yeah. I took piano lessons for two years." He said "two years" the way you'd say, "life sentence." "I used to bang away like it was a set of drums. Drove my mother crazy. You shoulda tried that with dance — stepped on a few toes, forgot how to count."

"Good idea," I said, smiling, but not at what he'd said. Both Fish and Stan had the same idea about what dancing was — either some leaper in tights or else a geriatric couple trampling all over each other's feet to big-band music.

They had no concept — the strength, agility, the focus ... the athletics of dance. The balance, the control you needed to hold a position without even the faintest muscle tremor. The way you got to hearing the music inside you even when there was no music being played.

Fish's beefy elbow brought me back to the present.

"There's Melody," he whispered in a voice reserved for NFL players and his beloved. "She really is ... you know, like a song. Hey! That's pretty good. Melody ... song? Maybe I should, like, write a poem, huh? Girls love that stuff."

"Go for it, big guy," I said, laughing.

"Hey, I got a soul." Fish pretended to look hurt, tripping me at the same time and almost sending me headlong. I twisted around and pushed him into the bank of lockers and just about had him pinned, but where I had agility, he had bulk. He pushed me back into the middle of the hallway, where I felt my heel connect squarely with someone's toe. A sharp scream punctuated the moment.

I knew before I even turned that with my mythic bad luck, it had to be Kat, though I couldn't remember having heard her scream before.

Sure enough. Those milky whites were smoking with rage, and probably pain.

"Could you watch where you're going?" she said through her teeth.

I figured I had three to four seconds before I turned stupid ... maybe more if I didn't look in her eyes. I lowered my head. Bad move.

"Try looking at my face for a change," she said sharply, crossing her arms across her chest. I felt myself redden, but I looked right into those eyes. And I was lost.

"Did I turt your hoe?" I asked.

A tiny smile flickered on her lips, which she almost immediately squelched. "Pardon?"

I shook my head. "Hurt your toe ... hurt your toe?" I said carefully, trying to focus somewhere in the safe vicinity of her nose.

"My hoe will be fine." She finally smiled. "What I want to know is this — are you as much of a pig as that Claude creep?" Her voice was soft, as if she wasn't trying to let everyone in on our conversation.

I shook my head back and forth, reminding myself suddenly of a wet dog. I stopped and tried to make everything inside me slow down. My palms were sweating and a vein was thumping in the side of my neck. Could she see it? "No," I answered in as deep a voice as I could manage. Sometimes it still cracked. "I'm not quite as much of a pig," I finished weakly.

She nodded and walked away, joining a group of girls and Fish, who'd apparently forgotten all about me. Then she turned just enough so that I could see that she had a little smile on her face. I decided this was a good thing.

"I'd say you're making real progress there, young Ben," Stan said, suddenly at my side in that under-cover-cop way he had of just appearing.

"She did smile," I said.

"Oh, yeah, you're in," he snorted.

As we moved up the hallway, I noticed someone else had witnessed the entire episode. And from the look on his face, Claude had heard the whole exchange. Great. One more reason for him to hate me.

—◦— ◦— ◦—

First class was history. I made my way to the back of the room, avoiding paper airplanes and outstretched limbs without incident. Stan had ducked out for a quick smoke, and I wondered if he'd make it to class. He spent most of his time — free and class — out in the courtyard, leaning against the stone wall in a cloud of white-blue haze.

The first time I saw Stan was in the playground at elementary school. It was Grade 2. He had a long stick in his hand and was waving it around like a pint-size Zorro. He had this bandana wrapped around his head, bandito-style, and his foes were imaginary because all the other kids were avoiding him. I'd watched for a while, edging closer, mesmerized by his fancy footwork.

After one really impressive flourish, I'd finally said, "I think he's dead."

Stan lowered the stick, cocked his head to the side. "I'm just practicing. To be ready."

I nodded as if I knew what he meant, which I didn't really, and suggested we play California kickball. And we've been friends ever since.

"Friends, Romans, countrymen, lend me your ears," Mr. Shepherd began, talking even as he entered the room. The classroom noise subsided marginally.

Aside from seeing *Dead Poets Society* one too many times, Mr. Shepherd was okay for a guy who had dedicated his life to reminiscing about the past.

"I'm sure you're all abuzz with the prospect of beginning our unit on Russian history." There was no response except for the odd groan.

"Believe me, when it all sinks in — the glory of St. Petersburg and Moscow, the horrors of the Revolution, the drama of the czars ... Russian literature — you will not be able to contain your enthusiasm."

He paused, it seemed, for some sign of life from the class, but receiving none, moved on. He went on about the glory of Russia for most of the class. I was checking my watch to see if it was still working when the bell finally rang, cutting him off in mid-sentence as he was blah-blah-blahing about how "there are no dead people in history ... their stories remain —"

The volleyball team was practicing after school, so I walked home alone. When I arrived at the back door, I paused, steeling myself for another "chat" with Aunt Frieda.

To my surprise, Mom was there, sharing a cup of tea with the old lady. It was early for her to be here, and I thought she looked relieved to see me.

"Ben," she said, rising to give me a kiss. "You're home early."

Usually I hung out with Stan until close to dinnertime because he hated going home. "So are you," I said.

"Aunt Frieda baked today. Try one of her cookies. They're peppermint." Mom's voice sounded cheerful enough, but her eyes were sending warning signals powerful enough to avert a shipwreck: Try one or die.

White, pasty lumps of cooked dough smeared with varnish-like icing gleamed from the kitchen counter. They reminded me of the provisions nuclear-war survivors were reduced to in science-fiction movies. But I could see from the crumbs on Mom's plate that she'd had one and was still breathing.

I took a small one. It was surprisingly light. "I had a big lunch," I said, laying the groundwork for being too full for more. I took a cautious nibble and met with a twang of sweet peppermint. Not bad. I popped the whole thing into my mouth.

"Hey," I said, grabbing three more. "These are great."

Mom looked relieved, and Aunt Frieda's eyes sparkled. "I'm glad you like them," she said softly.

"Really great," I repeated, going to the fridge for milk. "You should give Beth the recipe."

"I don't have a recipe. It's all up here," she said, tapping her forehead with a long, bony finger. Even her hands were wrinkly.

Her skin looked like a sheet that had been left in the dryer damp and scrunched, and as much as you tried to shake the wrinkles out, you finally had to resort to the iron because you'd promised you'd take the laundry out as soon as the timer went off.

"I said, how was school, Ben?" Mom asked slightly impatiently.

"Oh, uh, same. But I got tons of homework." I started to leave the room.

"Which subject?" Mom persisted, and I finally clued in that she wanted me to stick around.

"History," I said, leaning against the doorjamb. "Russian. Boring."

"Russian? Aunt Frieda lived in Russia for ... how long?" She turned to the old lady.

"Many, many years," Aunt Frieda answered. Then a faraway look came over her. "A lifetime."

"Maybe you could help Ben with his studying," Mom suggested.

I couldn't help shooting Mom an "are-you-crazy?" look.

"Nobody wants to hear an old lady's story," Aunt Frieda said, gazing out the window.

"Of course we do," said Mom, adding quickly, "and you're not that old."

Aunt Frieda faced us with a hint of a smile. "I'm not so old I don't know how old I am."

Mom looked a little flustered, but I knew what Aunt Frieda was saying. She didn't want anyone talking down to her. She said something about taking a little nap and left the room.

"I feel as if I'm always saying the wrong thing to her," Mom said, as soon as we heard the den door click shut.

"She's Dad's aunt, right?"

Mom nodded. "I'd only met her a couple of times, and then when your father died, I ... we lost touch."

"Was he, like, close to her?"

"I don't know ... I think so. His parents and Frieda's son, Jacob, helped bring her over when your father was little. She'd been separated from her son for quite some time before she was allowed to come to Canada. He — Jacob — was about your age ... maybe a little younger ... when he left Russia. It took years for them to find each other again."

"How do you just lose someone?"

Mom shrugged. "She's had a difficult life." She rubbed her eyes until I thought she'd rub the eyelashes right off. She always looked so tired. "She was kind to me, though."

"Huh? When?"

"I went to Saskatchewan to meet your grandparents just after Neil and I were engaged. The aunts, the formidable aunts" — she smiled — "threw a shower for me. After I opened all the presents and said my thank-yous — very politely, I thought — I started to clean up. I picked up the paper, you know, to throw it away. Suddenly the room went deathly quiet." Mom actually laughed out loud.

"What?" I asked.

"Well, it wasn't the Mennonite way to be so frivolous with perfectly good wrapping paper! I'd shocked the lot of them! But Frieda pulled me aside later and told me not to let it bother me."

I smiled uncertainly ... I didn't want to be a party pooper. "The, uh, Mennonite way?"

"Your father's family, Ben. They're Mennonites. You know that." She said this with her brows knitted together.

"I don't think so."

"Of course you do," she insisted. "You've forgotten." Then she looked at her watch. "I should get some studying in before dinner ... I have a class at eight." It occurred to me, as I watched her leave, how often she did that. Just when things started to get interesting, she'd walk out. It was as though all the parts of her were never in the room at the same time.

Aunt Frieda didn't come to dinner that evening. I wondered if she'd caught wind that feta omelettes with sundried tomatoes were on the menu. Mom

made some cream-of-chicken soup out of a can —
Beth looked personally insulted — and asked me to
take it in to Aunt Frieda. I'd noticed earlier that
Beth had scowled when she saw the peppermint
cookies too, but she tried one and finished the
whole thing.

I banged on the door with my elbow, holding the
tray awkwardly. When there was no answer, I put
the tray down and opened the door quietly.

She was sitting on the chair in the corner. I
placed the tray on the coffee table. There was no
movement of any kind, or any sound … not even a
snuffle. Just wax-museum stillness. I tapped the old
lady's hand gingerly. No response.

Then I remembered something I'd seen on a
television show. I looked around the room and
found a small mirror. Carefully I held it in front of
her face, angled below her nose, to see if it would
fog up with her breath. I stood behind her and
watched the mirror closely. At first all I could see
was her reflection from the nose down. No breath
fog. I was thinking about calling 911 or my mom
when Aunt Frieda awoke with a start, letting out
a yip of surprise to see the mirror dangling in
front of her.

I raised it quickly and came out from behind
the chair. "It's only me. I didn't mean to scare
you …" I was hot with embarrassment. I couldn't
tell if she was mad or what. "I didn't know if you

were okay … if you were sleeping or …" I felt like a complete idiot.

"Never put a mirror that close to an old woman's face! The wrinkles alone might give her a heart attack!"

"I'm sorry," I said again, but she chuckled, quietly at first, and then it turned into a rolling laugh until finally I had to join her. It really was pretty funny.

Eventually our laughter pulled the others in from the kitchen and they piled up in the doorway, peering in with worried expressions. This made us laugh even harder.

Aunt Frieda put her hand across her mouth. "I'm going to lose my teeth," she said, which of course made us laugh until tears were falling down our faces.

Eventually the others walked away and we sat there, recovering.

"Your soup's getting cold," I finally said, handing over a tissue for her running eyes.

As she took the tissue from me, her hand touched mine for a brief moment. "Thank you."

"No problem," I said. "You're okay in here?" Joni had done one of her murals on the walls — all gray and black with splashes of burnt orange — faces you could barely make out, with empty eyes and gaping mouths.

Aunt Frieda followed the direction of my gaze. She shrugged. "It's a little bleak, isn't it?"

"Yup … that's Joni." I shrugged. "A little bleak."

"I've noticed. It's quite different from the cards your father sent me."

I nodded. Dad hadn't sold many of his paintings. They were just starting to catch on when he died. Now most of them were piled up in the attic. Sometimes I went up and looked at them. They were watercolor landscapes mostly — recognizable — you knew what he was seeing.

"Still, she reminds me of him," Aunt Frieda said. "And so do you. Do you know how much you look like Cornelius?"

"Cornelius?"

Aunt Frieda smiled. "Neil. That's what your mother called him. We called him Corny."

I winced. "Corny? Oh man, poor guy." I sat down again. "I look like him?"

"Oh, very much. Especially your strong jawline."

"Huh. What, uh, what else?"

Her silver eyebrows knitted together in concentration. "You have your mother's build, I think. But the way you walk ... the way you move across the room — that's from your father. He could enter a room without anyone knowing he was there. I used to think it came from having no brothers and sisters, but that's not the case with you. Very graceful, he was."

"So you knew him pretty well?"

She nodded and her eyes drifted away from mine. "When I came to Canada, he was seven or eight years old. His parents sponsored me."

I nodded. My grandparents had died before I was born, so I'd never known them either.

"Did you and he, well ..." I coughed to loosen the tight feeling in my throat. "Mom doesn't talk about him a whole lot ... I don't know that much about him."

"Well, perhaps that's why I'm here," she said.

But before she could say anything else, Joni was at the door carrying a teapot. I could tell from the look in her eyes that it wasn't her idea.

"Come in, child," Aunt Frieda said, with a wave of her arm. "We were just admiring your work," she said, casting a glance at the wall.

Joni put the teapot down on the table. "Really?" she asked, then she looked embarrassed, sorry that she'd said anything. "Oh, thanks."

"Why don't you tell me about it?"

I took my cue and left the room. I was a little relieved. Even though I wanted to know more about my father, a part of me just wanted to leave him, like his paintings, up in the attic, leave all the old sadness up there.

━━ ━━ ━━

That night, right in the middle of a great dream about Kat, I woke up to the sound of "Lice, lice ... no, lice." At first I just lay there, waiting for Mom to come downstairs to see what was the matter. But there were no sounds of life in the house except for those whispers next door. I put my pillow over my head to block the sound. But I could still hear the word echoing inside my head ... lice, lice.

Finally I threw off the covers and went to the den. I pushed the door open. It took my eyes a while to adjust, but eventually I made out her small shape on the bed. Asleep, she looked even smaller. She whispered, "Lice," again.

I knelt beside the bed and took her hand cautiously. Her skin was as dry as paper. I felt her clench my hand, but she didn't wake up. What was going on in that dream?

Then her grasp relaxed. Her lined face turned smooth and the word fell away.

5

When I arrived at school the next day, I found a
pair of worn pink ballet slippers dangling from my
locker. I tore them off quickly and looked around
for the nearest trash can. As I stuck them inside, a
hand reached out, trapping my wrist between the
swinging door and the bin. I didn't have to look up
to know it was Claude. I could feel his dragon
breath over my shoulder. I twisted my arm free,
scraping it bloody.

"Hey, is that how you treat a present? You could
use them in your next performance," Claude said.
Arnie and Jeff, the goons, provided background
chuckling.

I avoided looking at my arm, knowing that the
sight of blood would only encourage these sharks,
but I could feel it, warm and sticky, clinging to my
ripped shirt.

"Yeah, well, they weren't my size, but thanks for
the thought," I said, trying to brush past Claude.

His arms shot out, pushing me against a wall of
lockers. Somebody's combination lock dug into
my back.

"Listen, I went to a lot of trouble to get those, and I want you to try them on, Ballerina Boy."

I tried to wrestle free, but Claude had twenty pounds on me. I was pinned and my arm was throbbing.

"What is your problem?" I muttered.

"I don't have a problem. You have a problem. So why don't you just stick your hand back in there and get ... the ... slippers, okay?"

My stomach heaved and I felt suddenly nauseous. Puking on his chest might be an effective way to escape, but I willed my breakfast down. Claude loosened his grip and pushed me over to the garbage can.

Then Jeff whispered loudly, "Teacher," and Claude sprang back like a hyena catching sight of a lion.

"Lucky break," he whispered, and the three of them were off.

Mr. Shepherd turned the corner in time to see them leave. His eyes traveled immediately to my bloody arm.

"What's going on here, Mr. Conrad?"

I held my arm across my chest. "Uh, garbage-can accident, sir."

"Let me see."

I drew my arm closer. "I'm fine."

But he insisted that I go to the nurse's office, even walking with me to make sure I went.

"Listen, Ben, I know that kid is trouble. But I can't help you if you don't tell me what's going down."

Going down. Like in a drug bust or a gangster hit. Why did teachers try so hard to be cool? If Shepherd had a clue about what was "going down," he'd know that ratting on Claude would be like wearing a sandwich board reading "Smash my face in with a wrench, please."

"There's no problem here, sir."

"Screw the 'sir,'" he said suddenly and angrily. I admit it — I was a tiny bit impressed with this response. For a millisecond he sounded like an actual person, not a data bank.

After we connected with the nurse, Shepherd hung around at the door. "If there's any more trouble, you come see me," he ordered, and then he was gone.

Nurse Shapiro disinfected my arm and wrapped it in gauze, muttering something about how I was lucky that I was up to date on my tetanus shots. When she was done, I thanked her and bent to pick up my knapsack with my good arm.

"These are dangerous times, Ben," she said seriously. "Don't be heroic."

I tried to laugh it off. "Tell the custodian to install safer garbage cans then."

But Nurse Shapiro just looked at me sadly.

At lunchtime, I paused outside the cafeteria before entering. Don't let Claude be there, I thought, then wondered where I was directing the thought exactly.

I felt a hand on my back, and my heart lurched.
I spun around.

"Hey, Ben." It was Fish and Stan.

"Whoa, judo move." Fish moved back a step,
arms in the surrender position. "What's with you?"

"You surprised me," I mumbled, pushing the
door open with my shoulder. I tried to hide my
bandaged arm. "I'm starving."

I avoided showing my arm until it was time to
carry the tray. It wobbled under the weight of my
food, with my wrist unable to balance it. I managed
to shift the food to my strong side, but by then Stan
had noticed.

"What's with the arm?" he said, as soon as we
found a table.

"I, uh, scraped it this morning," I said shortly.

"How?" He was staring at me, making it tougher
to come up with a plausible lie.

"I don't know how, exactly ... It was an accident."

Stan placed a finger on his temple. "An accident
you can't quite recall ... you blacked out right after
... can't remember a thing ... that kind of accident?"

"Exactly." I glared.

Fish waved his hands in the air. "The point is,
guys ... the point is, who cares? You should have
seen me at practice today." He spent the next ten
minutes talking about his near-Herculean efforts
on the volleyball court. Finally Stan broke in.

"So, basically, Fish, what you're saying is that
you're freakin' amazing?"

Fish smiled broadly, exhibiting portions of meat in his incisors. "Pretty much. But there are a few other decent players ... like that Kat. Whew, she's got some kind of serve. I can see why you like her, Conrad."

"I don't like her," I protested.

Fish's grin threatened to split his face. "Man, that's a load of crap," he sputtered.

"Geez, man, could you try swallowing some of your lunch," Stan complained.

"Sorry," Fish said good-naturedly.

I had a study and then photography after lunch, so I decided to ditch school and head home early. At least I'd have the streets to myself. As I left the chain-link gates of school behind me, a thought hit me. It's funny how some things can come on you suddenly and it's maybe the first time you've actually thought it, but it's like something you've known all your life. The world, I discovered, was not a kind place.

On the outside it looked okay — tulips pushing their way through the dirt, new leaves on trees. But just under the surface, the truth was, I lived in a world where a person could appear out of nowhere and shove you into a garbage can.

The kitchen was empty, and I was relieved to have the place to myself. Mom had left the stereo on, her surefire method to confuse potential burglars. I turned it off, preferring the silence. I decided to make myself a snack. The leftovers in the fridge were of the Beth variety — roasted squash stew, curry lentil soufflé and something covered in goat cheese that had overstayed its welcome. I snapped the lid back on quickly before more toxic fumes could escape and stuck it back in the fridge.

Then I noticed something on the far counter. Fresh buns. Only not Beth's fancy creations. These looked like little two-part snowmen: one large bun on the bottom topped by a smaller one, baked golden brown.

Such simple baking could only be the work of Aunt Frieda. I popped one into my mouth. They were delicious — not a seed or a speck of wheat germ to be found.

"They need butter, my boy," Aunt Frieda said from behind me.

"Good luck finding butter in this house," I said. "These are great."

Aunt Frieda frowned. "Let me see. I found some when I was baking the buns." She opened the fridge door to see for herself.

"It must have been prewar. Trust me, if it's saturated fat, you won't find it here. House rules."

"*Nah yo,*" she said under her breath, closing the door. "Is there a store close by?"

"A couple of blocks."

"Just let me get my purse."

Well, I was going to the store. I could imagine Mom's reaction if I let Aunt Frieda out on her own. I put my jacket back on with a sigh.

While I waited, I popped back a couple more buns. When she returned, Aunt Frieda was bundled up in a wool coat and little ankle boots, with a tam perched on her head and carrying a purse that must have been all the rage forty years ago. Lucky for me school was still in.

"You won't mind being seen with an old lady?" she asked, reading my mind. Man, she had sharp eyes.

"Of course not," I lied, but I made sure she couldn't see my face. I opened the door for her.

"What a polite boy you are," she said, as we walked out into the crisp, almost-spring air.

"Yup, that's me," I muttered. I was prepared to amble slowly alongside her, not for the quick pace she set.

"Uh, this way, Aunt Frieda," I said, pointing in the opposite direction. She spun around and marched up the sidewalk. I tried to think of something to talk about. Something we might have in common. Right, me and a hundred-and-ten-year-old lady.

"So, did you sleep okay last night?" I figured we had that in common, at least. Then I remembered her nightmare.

"Like a baby," she answered.

So, she didn't remember. I wondered if I should say anything, but I didn't want to upset her. It made me curious though. Why lice?

She stopped walking. "Aren't you supposed to be in school?"

"I, uh, I'm taking the afternoon off."

"How nice for you," she smiled, and I could've sworn there was a tinge of sarcasm there. Nah. Couldn't be. Not with that hat.

"I had to quit school when I was ten years old. My father thought I'd learned enough for a girl," she said.

"Really?"

"My mother needed me to care for the babies."

"The babies?"

"I had five younger brothers and sisters."

"Wow! Six kids under ten?" I let out a whistle. "And I thought we had a big family!"

She looked at me strangely. "And then there were my six older brothers and sisters."

I did the math. "Twelve ... twelve kids?"

Aunt Frieda nodded. She pushed the crosswalk button, and we waited for traffic to slow down.

"And the three babies that didn't survive."

My brain was shorting out. "Fifteen kids? You've got to be joking. What was she — a rabbit?" Oops.

But Aunt Frieda just chuckled. "Your father's father was my brother Benjamin. You were named after him." She smiled up at me. "He called me Fritzy."

"Was it too weird?"

She looked at me quizzically.

"Having so many brothers and sisters, I mean. Three sisters is bad enough."

"Sometimes my mother would stand at the end of the table — I never saw her sit at mealtimes — and I imagined her thinking, How on earth did this happen?" Aunt Frieda laughed out loud, and the tinkling sound made me smile.

"But we were never all together, of course. By the time the youngest had arrived, the older ones had already left home. Still, once you added the horses, cows and — oh, geese and chickens — we were quite a crowd."

"Horses and cows?" I asked. Was the old lady losing it?

But she nodded. "The family lived in the end of the house closest to the street and the animals at the far end. Sometimes, if a door was left open, you'd find a cow or a chicken in the living room!"

I laughed. "Guess there weren't too many health inspectors around, huh?"

"I remember one day finding a horse in the pantry eating *zwiebach*, those little buns I made this morning."

"Interesting."

"I didn't think you were interested in 'boring' history?" Her eyes twinkled.

"This isn't history ..." I started to say, but then I realized it was.

"Is that where we're going, *mein bengel?*" she said, pointing to the strip mall a block up the street.

"Beg your pardon?" Had she called me a bagel?

"*Mein bengel?* It means ... someone who is between a boy and a man, I suppose."

"In what language?"

"It's *pladeutsch*. You don't know any *pladeutsch?*"

I shook my head. "What is it?"

She seemed surprised. "*Ach!* Low German. Your father used to speak it quite well." She smiled. "Especially the vulgar words."

"Huh."

"It's the language spoken by some Mennonites."

There was that word again. I tried to look knowledgeable, but her next question nailed me.

"Do you know much about the Mennonite people, Ben?"

I decided that Mom's story about the wrapping paper probably didn't count and shook my head.

"Well, your father's people are Mennonites ... part of the religious movement started by Menno Simons?" She looked hopeful, but I shook my head.

"We began in Holland, then we lived in Prussia — that's Poland now — and eventually our people emigrated to Russia ..." Her hands were waving around as she spoke, and then she laughed. "This is clear to you?"

"Oh yeah, kind of like the horses and cows in the kitchen."

"*Nah yo*." She smiled. "When you are young, you care little about the past."

"No, actually I am interested," I said, and I was. I'd never thought of myself as belonging to "a people" before. I had a hard enough time seeing myself as part of a family.

"Well, my own story is not so large," she continued. "I grew up in a small village in the Molochnaya." Her gaze drifted away from me. "It was a beautiful place ... Our streets were straight as pins and lined with mulberry bushes and acacia trees. Our orchards, while we had them, were lush. We worked the land and we had prospered."

"I always thought ... huh," I stopped.

"You think of Russia as wartorn and chaotic?"

"Yeah, I guess." Vodka, I could have added, and leaking nuclear submarines, but I didn't.

"It is a beautiful country, Ben — my home for many years. But we kept mostly to ourselves. I suppose, deep down, we Mennonites are a wandering people ... never completely at one with a country. Our beliefs keep us separate."

"Beliefs?"

"We agreed to come to Russia because Catherine the Great promised that we would be able to keep our identity and speak our language — and worship our God. We would not be forced to fight in any wars."

"So, what ... you just sat on the bleachers and watched?" Maybe I didn't know much about Russian history, but I knew they'd never backed away from a fight.

"Oh, my boy, you're getting ahead of me."

"Sorry."

"*Nein*, I see your father's spirit." She reached up and ruffled my hair. "The peaceful years were short enough ..." Then she stopped, and I realized we'd arrived at the supermarket.

As I pushed the cart, Aunt Frieda dropped in items that hadn't seen the inside of our fat-free household for years: butter, whipping cream, sausages and bacon and a big bloody bag of chicken necks and backs. At the checkout, she pulled a worn change purse out of her World War Two handbag. Carefully she unfolded a twenty-dollar bill and handed it to the cashier.

The clerk learned closer and bellowed, "And fifty-four cents!"

Aunt Frieda nodded and handed over the change. The girl bellowed, "Have a nice day!"

Aunt Frieda smiled politely, but as we left the store she said with a shake of her head, "You know why old people go deaf?"

I shrugged.

"Because once you turn seventy, everyone yells at you."

We were crossing the parking lot when I caught sight of Claude and his friends standing outside a convenience store at the far end of the strip mall. I didn't think they'd seen us, and I casually turned, steering Aunt Frieda in the opposite direction.

She pointed up the street. "I thought we came from over there?"

"How about we take the scenic route home?"

"Nothing doing. If I don't get my bearings, I'll never find my way back here," she said.

I was going to have to come clean. "There's someone over there I'd just as soon not run into."

Her keen eyes peered into mine. "Are you in some kind of trouble, Ben?"

"Actually, I'm trying to avoid some kind of trouble. It's kind of complicated. You wouldn't understand."

Aunt Frieda followed along the not-very-scenic route. She was silent until we were on a side street, away from the main drag.

"I do, you know," she said abruptly.

"You do what?"

"Understand trouble."

I nodded, but I couldn't quite see it. She looked as if she belonged on a commercial saying that her soup was better than "store-bought." She was from another planet, and its orbit had no chance of intersecting with mine.

6

This "family dinner" thing was turning into a routine — choreographed, I figured, for the illusion of normalcy. The hot topic: Mad had scored her commercial. She was flying, practicing her Oscar acceptance speech as she put food on the table.

"And I'd like to thank my family ... well, most of them" — she paused to glare at Joni — "without whose support I would not be here." She sat down, smiling.

"You'd better thank me," Beth said. "All my creativity is channeled into the food that keeps you going."

"Not to mention the loins that pushed you forth into the world," added Mom.

"Please, not the loins," I pleaded. "Not at suppertime."

"Oh, Benny's blushing." Mad ruffled my hair.

I pushed the hand away. "I'd just like to get through one meal without some bodily function —"

"That reminds me," interrupted Joni. "I'm going on a colon cleanse tomorrow. Who's with me?"

At first there was no response. I mean, who in their right mind would volunteer for something so disgusting?

"Come on, you guys. Even as we speak, your colons are seizing up ... choking under the pressure of straining out the poisons and toxins of our diet."

"Hey," said Beth indignantly. "My food does not poison anyone."

Joni held up one finger. "Just a figure of speech, Beth. It's all the preservatives. Not your fault."

Beth looked slightly appeased.

"So, who's up for it?" Joni looked around the table.

I kept my head down over my food, shoveling it in.

But Mad, Beth and even Mom finally gave in. It was always easier to give in to Joni's demands than to fight her.

"How about you, Ben?" Joni persisted. "Your loins could use a little cleansing."

I shoved my unfinished dinner away. "A day of puréed spinach and wheat grass? Oh yeah, I'm in."

"Come on, Ben. I know you eat hamburgers and French fries at school," Beth added accusingly, like I'd been caught sniffing glue.

Thankfully the telephone rang.

"I'll get it," I said, leaping up from my chair.

I picked up the phone. "Yeah?" I saw Mom wince as I skipped the proper phone etiquette. "Hello?" I added.

There was no sound.

"Hello?" I repeated.

"Stay away from her."

"Who is this?" I demanded, knowing the answer.

"See ya at school, Ballerina Boy."

I put the phone down with a bang.

"Wrong number," I said.

Nobody questioned it, and soon the kitchen was throbbing with high-pitched voices. But I couldn't finish my meal, and as I carried the half-full plate to the sink, I felt Aunt Frieda's eyes follow me.

— ◆ — ◆ — ◆ —

I spent the rest of the evening in my room, trying to do homework. I read from the history text Shepherd had assigned, but the facts and statistics of the Russian Revolution blurred into a meaningless fog. I kept thinking about Claude. He wasn't the type to make empty threats. He had the kind of physique that made it easy to believe in evolution: thick, strong and hairy. It was rumored that he didn't own a neck.

So why was he picking on me? I was certainly no threat to him. Obviously he had a thing for Kat ... but that wasn't it, not completely. Ballerina Boy. My past coming back to haunt me.

I picked up an old photo of me, dressed in my Spanish matador costume. I'd been pretty excited about that dance. It was my first solo. And I'd danced well. I'd known it before the applause, before the judge's adjudication. I'd known that something amazing was about to happen as soon as the lights went down. Before I even heard the music, I felt it directing my movements. My body had known what to do instinctively, as though something was conducting me from the inside.

A sharp knock at the door broke through my thoughts, and I quickly hid the photo under my pillow.

"Yeah?"

"May I come in?" It was Aunt Frieda. I groaned. She was the last person I wanted to see.

"I'm, uh, studying," I said.

But the door creaked open anyway.

"You left without your dessert," she said, carrying a fluffy-moussy Beth creation. "I thought I'd return the favor from last night."

I wondered for a second if she'd known that I'd come into her room during her nightmare, but then I remembered the soup. "Oh, thanks."

Please go away — my brain tried to transmit a psychic message to her. But I was on the wrong frequency. She stepped into the room and sat down.

"That phone call after supper ... You looked pale."

Old Lady with Sharp Eyes. Stan and I used to play the naming game. We thought it up after we'd seen one too many John Wayne movies. I'd been Burps Good, for obvious reasons. Stan was Boy Who Never Laughs. Lately I called him Smokes Too Much.

"Just somebody from school," I said, loosely inside the truth.

"Some kind of trouble?" Was she playing the naming game? Then I remembered our earlier conversation.

"No, nothing like that," I lied.

Aunt Frieda nodded and stood. I thought she was going to leave, but then for a scary second I thought she was going to hug me again. But she reached down, picked up a book and held it at arm's length as she read the title.

"Russian history? You like this?"

"I don't know. It's just all so ... long ago, so ancient, you know?"

She flipped through the pages. "I was born just before the revolution."

Oh great, now I'd called her ancient.

"I, uh, didn't mean —" I started to say, but her laughter stopped me.

"What's history to you is for me ... a walk down memory lane. Isn't that something? Stalin is just a name to you — like Julius Caesar. But for me, he was a part of my nightmares for many years."

Nightmares. Lice. Could I ask her now? "Is that why ..." But then I chickened out. "Was it hard?" I asked instead. "The revolution, I mean."

"Everything was turning upside down. Our land was taken away. But that was also when I met my Henry." Her eyes softened when she said this name.

My eyebrows asked the question.

"My husband," she answered. "He was ten years older than I. He was with the White Russian Army, and he came home one time to visit his family. He walked past our house, and I thought he was so handsome. But too proud. He didn't even turn his head to look at me!"

She sounded so put out it made me laugh.

She smiled as well. "But years later — I'd just turned sixteen — he returned to the village to live. Now he was an official with the Red Army. I was working with my father when he stopped by to pay his respects. But Father was called away, and Henry stayed behind. He told me how grown-up I had become. But his look was far too bold — and I told him so!" She lifted her chin to a determined point.

"Do you know what he did then?" she asked, but didn't wait for an answer. "He picked a blossom from the cherry tree and placed it in my hair!"

She was obviously expecting a big reaction. "And?" I asked.

"Oh, *mein bengel*, young men were not supposed to visit a young girl without a parent present! And such vanity — to wear a flower!" But she smiled at the memory. "I took it from my hair and gave him such a scowl. He walked away then, whistling, but at the gate he looked back and saw that I still held the flower in my hand."

Right then, it wasn't hard to see the girl she must have been.

She added quietly, "We were married the following year," and left the room.

As I ate my dessert I thought about what she'd said. In my mind, I could almost see the village: the straight streets, the trees in blossom, the barn that was part of the house.

Later, when I heard her cry out, "Lice," I was surprised that she was having nightmares again, and I knew I'd heard hardly any of her story.

I went to her room and held her hand.

7

I considered contracting a disease the next day as a way to avoid school. Nothing life-threatening, just serious enough to require home tutoring for the next three months. A cold or a flu would only buy me a week at most, and something told me Claude's vendetta was not the quick-dying type. "Stay away from her," he'd said. Or what?

I knew what Mom would say if I told her about it. "Why don't you talk to him — ask him what his problem is?" As if. Sometimes I thought that my mother believed that all of life's problems could be handled like the papers she graded. This one's a B problem, this one's a C-minus. Sometimes I didn't think she lived in the real world with the rest of us — it was that frame thing. She preferred to patrol the edges.

Finally, I just got ready for school. There was no courage in my actions, but I knew if I didn't show up Claude would find his way to my house — and I didn't want him anywhere near my family.

I checked my back all the way to school. Every time a kid on a bike rode past or a dog barked, I jumped. I was relieved when I finally saw Fish and Stan at the front gate.

I'd been in one fight in my life. Grade 5. Horatio Jones had come up behind me and grabbed my Slurpee. I asked him to give it back, but he'd just pushed me down onto the gravel playing field. (See how well talking works, Ma?) Before I could even make a move, Stan had come steaming across the field and sent Horatio flying, Slurpee and all. He never bothered me again, but as I watched the cherry juice sink into the ground, I'd felt deeply ashamed that it hadn't been me who'd knocked him down.

Stan never mentioned the incident. That's the kind of friend he was, but I knew I couldn't tell him about Claude's phone call. Something in me would fizzle out if I handed my fight to him.

"Hey, Conrad." Fish waved me over.

"Practice over?"

"Yup, I was —" he began.

"Amazing?" I guessed.

"We are so lucky to hang with him," Stan said.

Fish grunted.

"No, really, Fish. It's like a privilege even knowing you."

"Yeah, yeah," Fish grumbled.

As we moved closer to the school, I looked around to see if Claude and his death squad had arrived.

"What's with you?" Fish said, poking me in the ribs.

"Me? Huh, nothing."

Stan looked suspicious. "Since when don't you join me in harassing Fish? It's one of our favorite things — like raindrops on roses and whiskers on kittens."

I smiled tiredly. "I didn't sleep that well," I said. After Aunt Frieda's lice rap last night, I hadn't fallen back asleep properly. Visions of black eyes and bloody lips had been dancing in my head.

"Hey, Fish. Nice serving today."

I recognized the owner of those smooth vocal cords immediately.

Kat walked up and joined our circle. I breathed in the smell of soap and something tangy — a citrus grove, I decided, on a hot summer day.

"Hey, Kat. Yeah, thanks. You too. You got a wicked spike," said Fish, straightening his shoulders. If he could have pulled off flexing his biceps without risking Stan's attention, he would have.

Kat just shrugged at the compliment, and her molasses-colored hair swayed slightly. I resisted the overwhelming urge to brush it with the tips of my fingers. I thought, if there'd been a cherry tree nearby, I might have plucked a blossom and put it in that hair.

Then I caught Stan checking me out. "You might want to watch your jaw. It's scraping the ground," he whispered.

"Shut up," I hissed.

Kat turned her attention on us. "Did you say something, Stanley?"

A wisp of smoke escaped from Stan's ears.

"It's Stan," he said tersely. "I was just having a private conversation here with my buddy Ben. It had entirely escaped me that I should ask your permission to speak. I do apologize."

Kat looked surprised at the sudden tirade. But I knew Stan well enough to know that anything could set him off, and he really did hate being called Stanley.

"Hey, how's your foot doing?" I blurted out. Okay, maybe it wasn't as smooth as Henry's blossom move, but I was trying.

It paid off. She actually smiled right at me.

"Well, I don't think it's broken," she answered, but her voice was higher than normal, registering at least moderately on the flirt scale. I recognized the tone from years of trying to make a telephone call and hearing Mad on the extension, mid-romance.

She swished her hair, another good sign. Then she turned and left.

Stan watched, then nodded slowly. "Huh. I think you are making progress, young Ben."

I grinned. Suddenly the world looked a half a shade brighter.

"No thanks to you, Stanley. You practically scared her off," said Fish.

Stan's eyes narrowed. "At least I wasn't making a play for her." He straightened his shoulders like a soldier, an obvious parody of Fish's earlier move.

"I wasn't making a play for her, Ben," he said. "I wouldn't do that to you."

"For the last time, there is nothing happening with me and Kat."

"I think you got a shot," Fish said, coming up beside me.

"It's true," said Stan. "You really are a likable chap."

"Why do you talk that way?" asked Fish, frowning.

"It's called reading," Stan explained with exaggerated patience. "You should try it sometime."

Fish rolled his eyes. He hadn't read a complete novel since Grade 4 and was proud of it.

"Philistine," Stan muttered, and left to go to his locker.

"Wacko," Fish said, as we watched him weave through the crowded hallway. "What's the Philippines got to do with anything?"

I smiled and slapped him on the back. "Absolutely nothing."

As we neared our lockers, I caught sight of Melody flipping her red locks in Fish's direction. "Go get her, boy," I said, and he was out of the gate like a greyhound.

I was still smiling when I got to my locker. The day was looking brighter — and that thing with Claude? Maybe he was blowing smoke. Maybe the phone call was just a stupid prank. But when I opened my locker door, a note fell out.

Claude was inspired this time — and artistic. He'd cut out a picture — probably mauled some dance program of his sister's. The male dancer held the ballerina high above his head in a lift, her arms opened in an arabesque. Claude had used a black felt marker to cross out the face of the male dancer. Subtle.

I pulled out the book I needed, slipped the note down as deep in my locker as I could and slammed the metal door shut so hard that the tips of my fingers went numb.

8

I skipped history and got home early, checking behind trees and jumping at shadows. By the time I walked up the cracked cement stairs to my front door, I felt about as brave as a fox on the day of the big hunt.

Aunt Frieda was in the kitchen doing dishes, and the smell of something good helped put Claude out of my mind.

"I have to say, I'm getting kinda used to this," I said, walking up to the pot, taking a peek. Sure enough, a bone that could've come from a small dinosaur bubbled amid a heavy sea of onions and vegetables.

"Meat!" I yelled.

Aunt Frieda jumped.

"Sorry, it's not exactly a familiar sight."

"I've noticed," she said, returning to the dishes. "How do they expect a boy to grow without meat?"

"Huh, lack of meat — maybe that's my problem," I said, picking up a tea towel. "You know, Aunt

Frieda, we do have a dishwasher."

"*Nah yo*. I like to keep busy," she answered.

I dried for a while, watching her ropy hands in the sudsy water. "What does that mean, *nah yo?*"

She dried her hands and moved over to the soup, adding bits of torn parsley and spices. "I'm not quite sure. 'Now yes,' I suppose, or, 'Well, yes.' It has a few meanings."

"Kind of like *aloha?*"

She laughed. "Maybe."

As I finished drying the dishes, my mind traveled back to the note. The ugly black marking was etched on my brain. You'd think a person would need a really good reason to hate someone as much as Claude seemed to hate me.

"How was your day?" Aunt Frieda's voice pulled me from my thoughts.

"Okay."

"Just okay?"

"Parts of it were good," I hedged, remembering Kat's smile.

"And the other parts?" she continued, undaunted.

But I didn't want to go into the other parts, not now and not with her. "Tell me more about Henry," I said instead.

She seemed surprised at this, but she turned off the element under the soup and sat down at the table.

"You're interested in an old woman's stories?"

"I have some time to kill," I teased, and she gave me a half smile. But it faded, and I could tell she was drifting back in time.

"Our wedding day was lovely. I wore my mother's dress. And carried violets. The political situation made it difficult — in the old days the entire village would have been invited. We would have cooked for days! But now things were different. Still, I felt very special. And the next day when we cleaned up, everyone said how much they had enjoyed themselves."

"The next day? What, no honeymoon?"

"An afternoon off work, perhaps."

"Oh man, you guys knew how to party!" I laughed, and she pushed my hand with hers.

"You have much to learn before you're a good Mennonite," she said.

I still couldn't get a handle on that one. The word made me think of farm plows and long black beards.

"We were happy, Ben. Henry continued his work as a government official, but it became more difficult for him. There was pressure from his comrades to join the party, but this he couldn't do."

"The party? Like, as in the Communist Party?"

"Yes. But to do so would have meant renouncing his beliefs."

"So why did he work there?" The look in her eyes made me wish I'd paid more attention to Shepherd's latest monologues in history class.

"At first he thought he could help our people more with an official position. There was such chaos — the land was being redistributed, and our people were not happy to give up what they had worked so hard for."

"I guess."

"But others said we'd grown rich on land that was never ours to begin with. It was a complicated time. Finally Henry decided he must resign …"

"So, he was unemployed?" I tried to fill in the gap as her pause lengthened.

When she spoke again, her voice was low. "One night I made borsht for him and fresh buns. I had good news. We were expecting our first baby. He was so happy, Ben. I'd never seen such a light in his eyes." She stopped again. I waited. "They came for him at midnight — stormed in through the doors. We were in our bedclothes."

"Who came?"

"Stalin's men. They took him to prison. Men with no faces, no eyes, no expression at all. Men of stone came. I did not see Henry again for years." Her lips formed a tight, narrow line.

"Why?" was all I could muster.

"Anyone with religious conviction was suspect. But there were no answers … no questions either, in such a state."

"What did you do?"

She looked at me as if she was considering her answer. I saw her take a breath. "I did not accept this, Ben. I wanted to tear at the soldiers with my hands. If I'd had a rifle I would have shot them right there in my kitchen. But Henry was shaking his head. He whispered to me, '*Liebchen*,' and his eyes were so full of love.

"They held him — he was across the room, but he touched the side of his head, the spot where he had placed the cherry blossom in my hair. And I could feel that touch. Then he was gone. I watched them take him away. I thought my life had ended right there on that night."

There were tears in her eyes.

"I'm sorry," I said. "I didn't mean to —"

She looked up at me. "No, no ..." She patted my hand. "It was a long time ago. But if you want to remember ... then you must relive the past."

It struck me when she said this, how feelings and memories flowed through her like a river. It was so different from my mother, who kept her memories wrapped tightly around her.

"I'm going to rest before dinner," Aunt Frieda said.

A thousand thoughts crowded into my mind as she left the room: horses walking into living rooms, chewing freshly baked buns; twelve laughing and crying children in one small house; tree-lined streets; men in army boots storming through doors, taking people from their warm beds Men of stone, she had said. Men with no eyes. Strangers with no reason to hate, who hated all the same. Claude.

The phone rang, but I let the machine pick up. I waited as Mom's neutral voice explained that we weren't available ... please leave a message at the beep.

I didn't realize I was holding my breath until I heard Stan's voice. "This is the truant officer. We've had reports that young Ben Conrad has been skipping —"

I grabbed the receiver and shut off the machine. "Hey."

"What's the big idea? You're cutting school more than me."

This was not true. Some of Stan's teachers wouldn't be able to pick him out of a police lineup.

"What can I say? You're a bad influence."

"You didn't miss much," he said, and in the background, I could hear yelling. Probably Stan's mom. She has the voice of a drill sergeant.

"Just a minute. I gotta move ... some guy's power raking outside my window." I could tell the hold button on his phone was being pushed. Stan didn't like to talk about what went on at his house. It got pretty ugly at times, that's all I knew. When he came back on the line, his voice had changed — quieter now and harder.

"Wanna grab a doughnut?" he asked.

"Yeah, sure." He needed to get out of the house. And I needed to avoid explaining why I was home so early. "Fifteen minutes."

— ◄ — ◄ —

Stan was waiting in the corner booth of the smoking section at Danny's Dunks when I arrived. The three butts in the ashtray told me he hadn't wasted any time getting there.

"What's up?" I asked.

He shrugged, lit up another cigarette. "Nothin' much."

"Éclair?" I asked, throwing my jacket on the ripped fake-leather bench.

He shook his head.

I bought two anyway, and a large chocolate milk, which I drained in two gulps. "Beth's having a coronary right now, and she doesn't even know why," I joked, taking a bite of one of the cream-filled doughnuts. But Stan didn't respond. Things must be bad for him not to want to talk about Beth.

For the next ten minutes we just sat there saying nothing at all.

"You sure you don't want it?" I finally asked, pointing to the remaining éclair.

"Nah," he said, blowing a long stream of blue smoke above my head.

I coughed. "You know, the nice thing about secondhand smoke is that it saves me the bother of having to take up the habit myself."

I didn't even get a half smile, but he did butt out the cigarette.

"They should just get a divorce," he said suddenly. "All she does is complain that he's never home, then when he shows up, she rags on him for never being there."

I'd only been to Stan's house a few times. The last one, we were sitting in his room, and his mother burst in without even knocking. She started in on him about his room, yelling as if I wasn't even there. It was the only time I'd ever seen him embarrassed. He never invited me after that.

"You think they might?" I asked.

Stan passed a cigarette between his hands but didn't light it. "Nope. They're stuck together. You know what they say — Love is war." He bared his teeth in an approximation of a smile, and I knew the conversation was over. "So, why'd you cut history?"

For a second I was tempted to tell him about Claude, but I knew he'd love to take it on. It wasn't that I was so thrilled to have a fight on my hands, but lately Stan's anger seemed to burn red through his skin. He had his own stuff to deal with.

"History's a drag," I said instead, although after the conversation with Aunt Frieda, this felt like a lie.

"I'm thinking of quitting."

"History? You can't change courses midsemester."

"School."

I didn't know what to say, so I finished the second doughnut. Stan looked dead serious. You're kidding? I could've said, but he wasn't. Why? I could've asked. But I knew the answer.

"Don't," I finally said.

"Why not? Give me one good reason." His eyes bored holes into mine.

Because I need you there, I almost said, but a guy didn't say that to another guy.

"What would you do?" I asked instead.

Stan's eyes moved down to the speckled Arborite table. He blew some stray ashes off. "Travel. You want to come? We'll go down to California or something. Maybe Mexico."

"Are you serious?"

"Ben, if I stay here, I think something bad's gonna happen. Something really bad."

"You can come live with us," I blurted out. I was crossing the line, but I didn't know what else to do. Stan's face slammed shut. He leaned back against the booth, lit another cigarette, drew in deeply.

"Forget I said anything." He shoved the pack of cigarettes in his pocket and stood. "I'll drop you."

We drove home in silence. All the way I tried to think of something to say, something that would make a difference. But what could I say that would change the fact that once he left me, he had to return to the battle zone. Love is war.

Stan's mom was wacko, my dad was dead. Stan's dad was there, but not really there. Kinda like my mom.

Fish had a happy family. If they were a sitcom, they'd be called that — the Happies. And like most people with happy families, he didn't even know it. He complained all the time: his mom didn't give him any privacy, his dad was too loud at soccer games. Stuff like that. It's kind of funny — people like Fish don't know what they've got and complain all the time. People like Stan and me … we know something's missing and we hardly talk about it.

"Come in for supper," I said, once we'd pulled up to my driveway. "The girls are grazing but my aunt made this great soup. You'd like her."

"Thanks, Ben, but I have stuff to do. See you around." He gunned the engine and tore off before I could even say good-bye.

I stood there until his car was a speck at the end of the street, thinking about how scared his eyes looked when he asked me why he should stay. Scared because maybe I couldn't give him that one good reason. And I couldn't, or I didn't. I knew I'd let him down. I knew it as soon as I'd seen his eyes turn blank. "No eyes, no expression at all … men of stone."

At first it seemed Aunt Frieda and I were going to have the borsht to ourselves. Joni and Beth had blended the colon-cleansing concoction — beets, cabbage, spinach, carrots, not to mention unidentified herbs and "purifying spices" — and despite being in long, elegant glasses, it looked revolting.

Mad was the first to glance longingly at our steaming bowls.

"How are your grass clippings?" I asked cheerfully.

Mad's eyes grew slitted and she took a gulp. "Yum."

"It's … invigorating," Mom said bravely, but she was checking out the tender piece of beef balanced on my spoon. I admit I held it out a little longer than necessary before putting it in my mouth. I groaned audibly for effect. Joni glared.

"There's plenty for everyone," Aunt Frieda said hesitantly, completely baffled at their meal of puréed compost.

"There *are* a lot of vegetables in it," Mad said quietly.

"Maybe just a little taste," Mom said, dipping her spoon into my bowl.

"Hey," I said, pulling it out of reach. "What about your colon?"

She ignored me and went to the cupboard for a bowl. Mad followed, and the two of them helped themselves to "a taste" — a full bowl each.

"Hmm, this is wonderful, Aunt Frieda. You should try it, Beth," Mad encouraged.

"I do have a soup class coming up …" Beth hesitated, looking at Joni. "Maybe I should try some … professional courtesy." She jumped up and filled a bowl.

Joni kept drinking her compost stubbornly until she'd finally drained the glass, then left the room. Aunt Frieda looked concerned.

"She's not happy unless she's suffering," I said.

Mom's spoon stopped midway to her mouth. "That's not true, Ben."

"Okay, whatever," I said.

There was an awkward silence around the table. Truth will do that.

Finally Beth spoke. "Could you give me the recipe?"

"She doesn't do recipes," I said.

"But I could show you," Aunt Frieda offered.

"That'd be great."

— ~ ~

I spent the rest of the evening in my room actually doing homework, but I kept thinking about Stan. Then I got to thinking about how Aunt Frieda's husband had been taken away, and I wondered, what made somebody turn to stone? I flicked through my history book and looked at the pictures of all the statues of men on horseback, men holding rifles, men sitting on rock-slab chairs looking down from great heights. Great men ... war heroes. What made a man a hero? Did all heroes end up carved out of great blocks of stone?

9

I had a hard time falling asleep, and after a couple of hours of tossing and turning I decided that grilled cheese was the answer.

I made the sandwich, added a couple of pickles and took it into the family room. Maybe there was a good late show on.

It took me a second to realize I wasn't alone.

Sitting in the ratty leather chair was Aunt Frieda. Her head was bent over one of our photo albums. She hadn't noticed me enter, so I whispered, "Can't sleep either?"

She didn't seem particularly surprised to see me and motioned for me to join her. The radio was playing something by Beethoven, I thought, recognizing not so much the tune but the sudden vivid picture of a dance routine I'd done once.

"Is this you?" She was pointing to a picture of me in my first dance costume, a pinstriped suit, a violin case beside me on the stage. Me as a seven-year-old tap-dancing gangster. I could feel the redness creep up my neck.

"Uh, yeah. Long time ago." I reached for the book, but she shook her head. She flipped a few more pages, pointing to another photo. Me again. This time in the Spanish getup, my first ballet piece. *Carmen*. I'd done it at the festival — came in first. I could still hear the music, feel the beat.

I picked up my sandwich. "Want half?"

"No thank you," she answered, still gazing down at the pictures.

"Do you mind if I turn on the television?"

She didn't respond, so I turned off the radio and flicked the television on. *Gilligan's Island*. Flick. A detective show. Flick. An infomercial. Flick. Another infomercial, but this one featured beautiful women, so I stayed for a while. "He'll never know they're not the real thing ..." A woman held up what looked like a small, transparent beanbag, and inserted it into her bra. Flick. I turned but Aunt Frieda was still looking at the album. I switched off the television.

"Why did you dance, Ben?"

"My sisters went, and Mom and I were always waiting for them. One day the teacher suggested I join in a few classes. Or maybe I asked if I could join. I don't remember."

"But why did you continue? There are so many dances, so many pictures here."

I shrugged. "I dunno."

"These pictures are so ... I'm not sure," she said, inspecting them closely. "I was reading about how

some cultures won't have their photo taken —
they're afraid that their soul will be captured and
... Look here." She pushed the book across the coffee table, pointing to me, midleap. I was grinning
because I couldn't believe I'd nailed it. "I believe
that's true in your case." She looked up, right into
my eyes and I looked away.

"I should get to bed," I said.

"I always wanted to dance," she said, stopping
me in my tracks.

"You mean, like on stage?"

Aunt Frieda looked shocked. "Oh, my. *Ach.*"
Then she laughed. "Imagine that. No, I meant, I
wanted to try ... just try."

"You mean you've never danced?" My turn to be
shocked. "As in ... never?"

"When I was growing up, dancing was a sin."

"Kinda like how my sisters dance," I joked, but
she was serious. "Really, like an actual sin?"

"Oh, yes. Along with card playing, smoking and
drinking. All tools of the devil."

"So what did you do for fun?"

"Well." She stopped to think. "We played games
and laughed with one another, but fun wasn't an
everyday occurrence."

"Huh."

"Look at this picture here. Look at your smile."

I peered over her shoulder. I was twelve in that
photo. It was my last year of dancing. I was

dressed like Aladdin, and sure enough, a big grin stretched across my face. "Seems like a long time ago," I said. "I was just a kid."

"So many costumes. You must have been very good. Why did you stop?"

"I outgrew it, I guess."

She closed the book but kept it on her lap with her hands folded on top. "When I was young, at harvest time, the Russian peasants would come to our village to help gather the fruit. At night there would be bonfires and music. I remember sneaking out of my room one night — just little, I was — drawn by the firelight. I stayed in the shadows and watched as they played music and danced. There was one couple — a man and a woman — singing together with such feeling, I was filled with ... longing. As though I was grasping for something that was in my soul but beyond my reach."

Part of me just wanted to slink out of there while her eyes were closed. But the other part knew exactly what she was talking about. The difference was, I had known the thing that was inside of me — and I'd pushed it away.

"How come I wasn't invited to the party?" Mom asked, entering the room looking bleary-eyed.

"Insomniacs only," I answered. "Did we wake you up?"

"I was looking at some of your photo albums, Catherine. I hope you don't mind."

"Not at all, Frieda. We want you to make yourself at home here," she said, but her voice sounded stiff.

"You've been so kind to me — all of you, to let me into your home."

Mom didn't say anything, so I did. "We like having you here. Right, Mom?"

Mom snapped out of her daze. "Of course we do. Of course."

Aunt Frieda's keen eyes narrowed, but all she said was, "I'm going to take this old body to bed. Good night." As she passed by, she stooped and gave me a kiss on the top of my head. It surprised me, but I didn't mind.

Mom watched as she left.

"She's very fond of you, Ben. I really appreciate the time you've spent with her."

"Actually, I like her."

"I can see that." Mom put the photo album back on the shelf.

"Are you glad she's here?" I asked.

"Of course."

"You don't sound sure," I persisted.

"Sometimes it's difficult, Ben."

"What is?"

"The past."

"You don't talk about it ..."

Mom looked away. "I think about it, about him ..." she began, but then blinked twice, hard. "I've tried

to keep things together, Ben. It hasn't been easy."
She sat up straighter. "There wasn't ... a lot of money
after he died."

"I know," I said, disappointed at where the
conversation had gone but hardly surprised. "You
should go to bed," I said. "Don't you have a big test
or something?"

She squeezed my arm, the one Claude had
mangled, and I winced.

"What's wrong?"

"Nothing. Tennis elbow maybe."

"You're playing tennis now? That's good," she
said absently. "Are you okay here?"

"Yeah. I'll go to bed soon."

She bent down and kissed my cheek, and then
she was gone. The house was still.

I flicked the television back on. A rerun of
The Brady Bunch flashed up. Six, eight, nine
smiling faces popped onto the screen, each in
a neat box. Cheery singing broke the silence of
the room. I couldn't stomach the peppy music,
so I turned it off when they got to the part
where they were "living all together, but they
were all alone."

I could relate. All alone in a house full of people. Joni probably felt that way too. Even Mom.
Ever since Dad died, it was as if a big hole had
been blown into the side of our house, and

nobody could figure out how to fill it. I wondered if Aunt Frieda had felt that way when they'd taken Henry away.

～ ～ ～

It was noon by the time I even considered crawling out of my blankets on Saturday. Then Mom came into my room holding the telephone. She had her hand over the receiver.

"Ben, it's Mrs. Belado. She wants to know when you last spoke to Stan."

I sat up. "Yesterday afternoon. Why?"

"Did he say where he was going?"

Mexico. California. I shook my head. "He didn't say."

"I'm sorry, Marion." Mom spoke into the phone. "Ben hasn't seen him since yesterday afternoon. No, he didn't ... I'm sorry. Yes, well, let us know."

"What's up?"

Mom sighed. "Stan didn't go home last night. They have no idea where he is. Are you sure he didn't mention anything to you?"

"Not really."

Mom straightened like a golden retriever catching sight of a bird. "Not really or not at all?"

I pulled a sweatshirt over my head. "You know how things get over there. He was bummed ..."

"And?"

"He said something about Mexico, but he wasn't serious. At least I didn't think he was."

Mom was already punching numbers into the phone pad. As she left the room, I could hear her telling Stan's mom what I'd said.

I went to the kitchen and poured myself some cereal. Mom sat beside me.

"Things really are quite bad over there, aren't they?"

I nodded.

"Marion and Alan have some problems to work out, Ben."

"*Some* problems?" I stared at her.

Mom looked uncomfortable.

"I've known them since Grade 2, Mom. They fight all the time. They throw things."

"You'll call them if he contacts you," she said. It was as if she hadn't even heard what I'd said.

"Sure."

"I have to get to school. I'm running late." But at the doorway, she stopped. "You know, Ben — maybe it isn't the best time to say this, because I honestly hope that Stan is all right ..." She looked uncertain about continuing.

"Yeah?"

"It's just that I don't think Stan has been the best influence on you." The words came out quickly.

"What do you mean?"

She scratched her forehead. "He's just so troubled ... always has been. Of course I've let you choose your friends, but ..." Again with the pause.

"But?" I prodded.

"He seems like a loose cannon, okay? As if he could go off at any moment. And I don't want you to get hurt."

I took a breath, a deep one. "He's unhappy, Mom," I said slowly. "Some people can admit they're unhappy." I looked right at her.

She blinked a couple of times, and she might have swallowed, but other than that … nothing. "So you'll call his mother if you hear from him."

I didn't even bother to answer. She left the room for her world of facts and figures and grade-point averages, where everything made sense. But the real world didn't make sense. You'd think that she, of all people, would know that. And maybe deep down she did. Maybe she'd just given up when Dad died.

— — —

I decided to walk over to Fish's to see if he'd heard anything from Stan.

"Go on in, Ben," his mom said at the door. "He's still in bed. Can you believe that?"

"Disgraceful."

Sure enough, Fish was sawing logs when I crept into his room. I pulled the pillow slowly out from underneath him and watched his beefy head slide onto the sheets. I stood back, having shared enough sleep-overs with him to know what would come next.

His eyelids fluttered, then he groped around for the pillow. Suddenly he was wide awake, flapping his arms like an overweight duck trying to take flight. "Huh, what ..." He sat upright, flung his legs over the side of the bed and blinked. Then he saw me, grinning down at him from across the room. I flung the pillow at him.

"Geez," he groaned, falling back down on the bed. "What are you doing here?"

I slid down the wall to the floor. "Stan's mom called this morning. He didn't go home last night."

No sooner were the words out than Fish's mom came in, holding the phone, doing a repeat performance of my morning.

After we'd established that no one had heard from Stan, Fish's mom left.

"Where do you think he went?" Fish asked, pulling on some clothes.

I told him about our conversation the night before. "You don't think he meant it, do you?"

Fish shrugged. "You never know with him. He's always been a little crazy. Remember last year when he spent the night in my tree house and I found him in the morning?"

We looked at each other, then headed out.

But the tree house was deserted. We climbed up using the weather-beaten rope ladder and onto the platform — "the lookout" we used to call it. But it barely held the two of us anymore.

"Seems like a long time ago when we used to come up here," Fish said.

But it had only been a couple of years. Stan and I had met Fish on the first day of Grade 8. A trio of shrimps, scared to death of a big school after the safe smallness of elementary school. Since then we'd grown a foot, didn't fit the old places. Still, I could imagine what brought Stan back here last year.

"I kinda feel we might not see him again," I said, looking out across fences, garbage cans and the horizontal line of the backyards of Fish's neighborhood.

"He'll be back. He just needs some space. It's not that bad over there, is it?"

As far as I knew, Stan didn't talk about his home life with Fish. Just me, once in a while.

"It's bad."

Suddenly the cramped tree house felt creepy, and we left. We spent the rest of the day checking out places he might have gone: the arcade where he was reigning king of the universe, the bowling alley where he liked to smoke and jeer at bowlers — the ultimate loser sport, he called it — and Danny's Dunks, but with no luck.

It was dusk when we sat down on the curb, neither of us saying anything. The streets were dull with the changing light. We'd grabbed lunch at the bowling alley, and it was still sitting there in a lump in my intestines. I couldn't even remember what I'd eaten.

"Where next?" I asked.

Fish shrugged, checking his watch. "Melody said there was this party down at the lake. Want to check it out?"

"Maybe," I said, unsure.

"There's nowhere else to look, Ben."

"I guess."

"I think Kat's gonna be there."

I pretended to ignore this. "I just hope he doesn't do anything stupid."

Fish got to his feet. "He's a big boy."

We walked over to the sky-train station a block down the street. Luck was with us — a train was pulling up as we climbed the steps to the platform.

"You know where you're going?" I asked.

"Always," he said, stepping into the half-empty train car.

Typical Fish. Even if he didn't know exactly where he was going, where he ended up was where he'd say he meant to be. It was an art form, really, the way he got through life.

"Who's going to be there?" I asked, sitting across from a guy who smelled like he'd last bathed Tuesday of the previous year.

"Some of the guys from the soccer team, I think. Don't sweat it, Conrad." Fish smiled over at the guy, who offered him a piece of the cantaloupe he was eating with a plastic spoon. Fish just shook his head pleasantly.

Fish, unlike Stan and me, had about five or six groups of friends that he bounced back and forth around. Everybody liked him. And I could tell he was eager to be around more people right now. He was like a dog that way — liked to move in a pack. But anytime I'd been included with his other friends, I felt out of place. I could see him change like a chameleon. It didn't matter when Stan was around — we'd just drift off and catch up with Fish another day. But Stan wasn't here, and I didn't feel like going home yet.

At the beach there was only a handful of people, but Fish scoped out the ones he knew. I tagged along as he rushed to greet them, moving tall and sure across the pebbly beach.

"You guys remember Ben, right?" Their eyes skimmed me quickly, blankly. "Andrew ... Jamil."

I nodded, grunting hello.

"Care for a beverage?" Andrew moved to the edge of the woods where a cooler sat, cleverly disguised as a molting shrub.

"Great camouflage," I said, taking a can of soda. Fish grabbed a beer, downed it in one stream and crushed the can, tossing it into the trash can.

"I hear you're a ballerina," Andrew said, smirking sideways at Jamil.

"Used to be," Fish said, attempting, I guess, to defend me.

"Male dancers aren't called ballerinas," I informed them, resenting having to explain myself ... again.

"Sorry. My mistake," Andrew said, wandering off with the smirk plastered on his face.

I felt my skin twitch across my face as I tried to keep a neutral expression. But it reminded me too much of Claude, and I wondered if I'd always be a target for idiots.

"Mel's here," Fish whispered excitedly. "And Kat. Let's go over there."

"In a minute. You go."

"You sure?" he asked, but he was already on his way.

Someone had cranked up the music. I moved over to a log and watched from a distance. Fish's lope turned into a swagger the closer he got to the girls. Something about the magnetic force field, I figured. He really was something to see. You could throw him into a tank full of sharks and he'd have them synchronized swimming within thirty seconds. He was charming. He fit. I'd never seen him flustered during the entire time I'd known him, except maybe with Stan.

I had a good view of Kat. She was wearing jean shorts and a rusty-red sweatshirt with bright white socks that stood out against her long, tanned legs. She was so pretty it made my teeth hurt.

People were starting to dance. It was a good song, and I could feel myself respond to the music.

It should be so easy to walk over to Kat, ask her to dance. I mean, that was one thing I knew how to do.

So do it, I told myself. Ten, twelve steps and I'd be there. I could ask her ... or maybe just take her elbow, and lead her to the clearing. I could take her in my arms — it was a slow dance now. The moon was almost full, a dimpled path of silver light spread out across the water.

You're such a good dancer, she might say.

Maybe I'd move into one of those Fred Astaire routines we'd learned at the academy. The girls always said I was easy to follow.

Where'd you learn those moves?

I wouldn't have to say anything ... just let our bodies follow the beat, my hand on her back. Maybe I'd try a dip at the end — or would that be overkill? Maybe I'd try to kiss her ...

Mid-daydream, I noticed she was looking back at me. How long had I been staring? She probably thought I was stalking her. I lifted the can up, drank long until the soda was gone, except for the part that splashed up to the bridge of my nose. Very cool. I wiped my face with my sleeve and when I looked again she was gone.

I craned my neck, standing to see where she was. Then I saw her. She was dancing. At the edge of the group, by herself, it seemed. Her body moved slowly, unselfconsciously, and the wind lifted her hair, blowing it softly across her face. She pushed it back with one fluid motion, smiling.

I looked around but there was no one behind me. It was entirely possible then, that she was smiling at me! As coolly as I was able, I let my eyes find her again. Now her back was to me. I wondered if she knew I was watching. I should go to her — I knew that. But I also knew I wouldn't. What if she laughed at me? She wouldn't. What if I tripped? I might. What if I just got over to her and somebody else stepped in — somebody a whole lot better looking. Somebody a whole lot more cool. Highly likely.

Her body moved with the music, and she looked directly at me. She smiled again, but it was more tentative this time. As if she wasn't sure. And I turned — turned and walked away.

By the time I reached the trees, I felt someone behind me, and then a hand brushed my shoulder. I checked hopefully, but it was just Fish.

"Where are you going? The party's just starting."

"I'm not much in the party mood," I said. "You want to come to my house?"

Fish squirmed. "Man, everybody's here."

"Yeah, you're right. But I'm gonna go."

"You sure?" Fish asked, but I could tell he was itching to get back to the action.

"Yeah."

I watched him rejoin the group. Within seconds he was dancing jerkily, like a guy who forgot his sandals on the hottest day in August. He really looked out of place on a dance floor, but it didn't seem to matter. Then it occurred to me that it wasn't wrong for a guy to dance — just to dance well. It was okay to dance, but not to be a dancer. Or maybe it was more personal than that. Maybe it was just wrong for me. Maybe there was a big red cosmic arrow pointing at me: attack.

As I watched, Fish moved in his distinctive style, closer to Kat. He said something to her, and she laughed. He made it look so easy. My stomach clenched like it was about to be hit, and I could taste something bitter, metallic, in my mouth. I couldn't watch anymore. I walked back through the darkening woods up to the street.

Fish was ... Fish. Fun to be around and living proof, in a way, that I wasn't a total loser. But he was like one of those imaginary friends you have when you're little — it had more to do with what you hoped for in a friend than what actually was. If I tried to picture him and me twenty years from now, just shooting the breeze together, I couldn't. Fish was a now friend.

But Stan was the real thing — and he was gone. I could still see him in Grade 2 ... with that bandana around his head and his tree-branch sword. He was still out there somewhere, fighting invisible enemies.

━ ━ ━

I was at the kiosk, buying my ticket for the sky train when I noticed a guy, maybe a year or two younger than me, hunched over in the corner with his back to me. I had to pass him to get to the escalator, and when I did I could hear him breathing really heavily, as if he was crying. I almost ignored him but turned back before my foot hit the first moving step.

"You okay?"

No answer.

"Buddy, you okay?" I moved so that I could see his face. It was red and blotchy, even in this shadowy light.

He cleared his throat. "Some guys ... they, uh, took my money. I can't get home," he managed to get out.

He was really scrawny, dressed only in a pair of shorts and a T-shirt that looked like it had been through a couple of older brothers.

"They took my jacket, too." Then he stopped and took another deep breath.

I dug through my pocket, pulled out a crumpled five. "Here, take this."

He looked down at the money, reaching for it slowly. Then he put it into the machine to buy a ticket. He offered to give me the change, but I shook my head.

"You might need to make a call. Don't worry about it." I stepped onto the escalator and he followed.

"I, uh, got these allergies, you know?" he said quietly.

"Yeah, pollen's bad this year," I said, not knowing if the pollen was good, bad or nonexistent.

The guy sniffed once more, but he seemed to be getting it together. Before long a train pulled up and we walked inside. He sat beside me until it was his stop.

"You okay?" I asked, as he stood to leave.

He looked uncertainly out to the cheerless platform but nodded. "I live close by. Hey, thanks."

"No problem," I said, as the door closed behind him.

I saw my reflection in the window, blue and transparent ... like you could almost see bones and muscle and blood moving around.

The guy just got mugged, and he tried to pretend his allergies were making him cry. I tried to remember the last time I'd cried. I couldn't. Probably back when I was a kid and stubbed my toe or something. Something small, but crying always seemed to make it just a little better. At least it was a way to say, Hey, getting hurt really sucks. Hey, look at this, I'm wounded here ... I'm suffering. I wondered what I'd do if some guy grabbed me, took my money, my jacket. Would I pretend I had allergies? Probably.

As the train sped along toward the narrow bridge that spanned the river, all you could see on either side was an expanse of black sky and below the even darker water. It was as though we were moving headlong into nothing, and suddenly I was angry.

I was angry at the faceless guys who'd beaten that guy back there. At Fish for dancing — *dancing* with Kat when I couldn't. Angry at Stan for taking the easy way out and angry at myself for having to go back home where I wasn't needed.

The train reached the end of the line. If I didn't move, I'd just end up back where I'd already been.

10

I spent the rest of the night channel surfing and hoping Stan would call. But there was nothing.

Then at eleven o'clock the phone rang.

"Hello?"

Silence.

"Stan, is that you?" I sat upright in the chair.

"Yeah."

"Where are you?"

"Outside town. Some truck stop."

"What are you doing?"

"Driving, mostly ... thinking about coming home."

"Do it."

"I need a reason, Conrad. Just one."

"It's just" — I struggled for the right words — "better when you're here, Stan. Honest to God."

More silence, then a chuckle. "Gosh, you miss me."

"Somewhat," I said, and he laughed. "Call your mom, Stan. She's been phoning all over town." I felt a bit bad about saying this, since as far as I knew she'd only made two calls, but still.

"Really?" he asked. He sounded like a kid, hopeful.

"Really," I answered.

"Maybe I'll do that."

"And call me when you get home."

"Sure."

"I mean it."

"Yeah, okay ..."

"Okay."

"Conrad?"

I waited.

"Thanks," he said, his voice barely a whisper. And then the phone went dead.

I felt as if somebody had just rolled a boulder off my chest. I flicked the television off and went to tell someone. The girls were all out. Saturday night, what did I expect? Mom was still at the library, according to a note on the table. I peeked inside Aunt Frieda's room, but she looked like she was dozing over her big black book. I went back to the living room.

I turned on the stereo, and music filled the corners of the room. All those years of dancing had made it impossible for me to listen to music without my body responding in some way — that's why I didn't much listen to music anymore. But now, it was like somebody had given me a shot of adrenaline, and I could feel the Latin beat right down to the soles of my feet. "The sole of your foot," Miss Fleur would say. "The *soul*," she'd repeat, in that irritating way she had, to make sure you hadn't missed her amazing pun.

I pushed the sofa to the side of the room and, using it as a substitute barre, did some hamstring stretches. As the muscles warmed up, I wondered if I could still pull off a triple pirouette. "A dancer's limbs ... extend into infinity ..." Miss Fleur must have said that a million times. I reached as the words echoed inside me. "Always up." I reached higher and turned ... once, twice ... and remembered that place that was in between time ... the place that extended to infinity.

In the middle of the third turn, I felt someone's eyes on me. Aunt Frieda, in her slippers, stood in the doorway. She clapped her hands and grinned.

I stopped, suddenly awkward.

"Oh, no, keep going. It looks wonderful."

I hesitated, but the sparkle in her eyes inspired me suddenly. "Actually, Aunt Frieda, I hate to dance alone and, I think" — I leaned into the music — "that this is our song."

Now it was her turn to look awkward. Panicked, actually. "No, *nein*, I couldn't," she said, backing up a couple of steps.

"It's easy. I'll show you."

I did a couple of simple steps. Your basic slow-slow-quick-quick routine. She didn't move, but when I reached for her parchment-paper hands, she didn't resist either. At first she moved like a plank of wood, straight up and down.

"Find the music," I urged.

We did a slow foxtrot, but she moved stiffly, as if she was on the bow of a boat in rolling waves.

"Just climb right into the music and stay there until you feel it."

Gradually I could feel her fragile form relax, and I knew the beat was penetrating. I heard Claude's taunting — Ballerina Boy. What would he say about this scene? But then Aunt Frieda laughed.

"I'm dancing," she said, awed.

I pushed Claude out of my head.

"And now the corner step," I said. "Just follow my lead." I moved forward a step, then back one and we did a half turn. Aunt Frieda followed without missing a beat.

"You're pretty good," I said, impressed.

She smiled but didn't say anything. She was concentrating on the steps. When the song was finished, I bowed. "Thanks for the dance."

"Oh, my," she said, moving over to a chair and sitting down. "My, my. That was ... fun."

"Yeah." And it was.

"You need to keep dancing, Ben," she said, suddenly stern and grandmotherly.

"I thought it was a sin."

But she didn't smile. "Perhaps in your case it would be a sin not to dance."

That's when I noticed Mom standing in the doorway. I wondered how long she'd been there.

"Oh, Catherine, come in. Your son was just

teaching me to dance — could you ever have imagined such a thing?"

Mom walked over to the stereo and turned down the music. Not off, just down. Her face was creased with tiredness. She smiled limply. "You don't mind?" she said, pointing to the stereo. "I've had such a day. I think I'll go straight to bed."

Aunt Frieda started to get up. "I've baked some strudel. Why don't I make you a nice cup of tea before you go to bed."

Mom's eyes crinkled up at the corners. "That would be lovely." She sounded grateful.

I tried to remember the last time anyone offered to make her a cup of tea and I couldn't.

Then the door flew open, and the twins piled in, chattering in tandem, as usual.

"Ooh, good song," Mad said, flinging her cape onto the couch. "I must dance. It is in me. C'mon, Benny Twinkletoes." She held her hand out.

I shook my head. "Uh-uh."

Aunt Frieda looked at me, a question in her eyes, but I looked away.

I couldn't dance. My sisters'd just nag me to take it up again. What happened tonight wasn't about that. I was just being nice to an old lady who'd never danced before. That was all. It had nothing to do with my life.

"I'm tired. I'm going to bed."

The twins looked disappointed. Until Beth yipped as she spotted something in the kitchen.

"Strudel!" she yelled. "Aunt Frieda, you didn't." She sounded as excited as if one of her Firemen Calendar men was sitting on the counter waiting for her.

"I need to know how you did this!" she hollered from the kitchen.

"I'm coming," Aunt Frieda answered. "You'll be all right?" she said to me.

"I'm fine."

The noise in the kitchen rose as both Beth and Mad tried to out-twin each other. My feeling of lightness slipped away.

11

Sunday morning arrived earlier than usual. Maybe not technically, but the smell of fresh baking pulled me out of bed long before I was used to getting up. As I grabbed a pair of sweats, it occurred to me that it had been years since I'd seen 8:30 on a weekend.

I felt like one of those cartoon characters being dragged along by an aromatic waft in the air as I made my way to the kitchen. But the sound of voices stopped me before I entered.

"... such a good dancer, Catherine. The look on his face last night was so —"

"I'm not saying he's not talented, Frieda, but I'm a little surprised to hear you championing the cause of dance. I didn't think dance was big with Mennonites." That was Mom.

Aunt Frieda said something that I couldn't make out. I leaned forward.

"I suppose," said Mom. "It's just that I worry about him. He needs to focus on his grades. He can't throw away his future. It hasn't been easy to be both mother and father, you know."

"I know, dear. And you've done a wonderful job."

A clatter of coffee cups and then, "I don't know about that ..." More clatter of dishes. What were they doing? Playing Frisbee with them? How was a guy supposed to eavesdrop with so much noise.

"He's still a boy, Catherine."

"It's different now. Things are different. You don't know how much he was teased for being in dance. It hurt him, I think. And it's dangerous out there ... Kids carry weapons to school." Her teacher voice.

"Men have always carried weapons."

There was a silence.

"I know you survived a war, Frieda. But this is different. Ben is different. He's ..."

I could hear my heart in my ears.

"He's sensitive," she finally said. "He's not a fighter, and that's what you need to be to survive."

My appetite disappeared. I didn't stick around to hear Aunt Frieda's response. I went back to my room and closed the door tightly behind me.

My own mother thought I was a wimp ... a weakling ... that I didn't have what it took to survive. Like she was some big expert. Why did she even think she knew me? I felt the anger uncurl inside me. She was always in the library or teaching or grading papers. She didn't have a clue who I was. Plus, me living in this dormitory for women — what did she expect?

I pulled a T-shirt on and changed into running shorts. I needed to get out of here.

I almost made it to the front door.

"Ben, can you come here for a minute?"

"I was just going for a run, Mom."

"Perfect," she said. "That's a good idea."

"Yeah, figured I could use some toughening up."

But she didn't flinch, didn't make the connection.

"Would you mind walking with Aunt Frieda to that church at the corner of Pine and Sixteenth? It'll only take ten minutes or so."

Did I really need a ten-minute walk with Eyes That See Everything? "Whatever."

"Ben."

"It's okay, Catherine," Aunt Frieda interjected. "It's not far. I'm sure I can find my way. If not, I'll just wander around, and hope someone takes pity on me. I'll take my medication with me just in case."

I couldn't help it. I had to laugh. "Okay, I give up."

Her eyes sparkled. "I'll just get my purse."

Mom sipped her coffee thoughtfully. "You two have an interesting relationship."

I shrugged. "She says what's on her mind. I like that."

"Yes she does." An expression I couldn't read crossed her face. "Ben?"

"Yeah?"

"I, um … we could …" She stopped and cleared her throat. "Thanks. I appreciate this."

"Okay." I wondered what she'd really been about to say.

"Well, I'm ready." Aunt Frieda appeared, coat and hat on, with her purse dangling on her arm.

As we left the house I told her that she looked good.

She tossed her head with a look something like disbelief, but she seemed pleased. "I used to be considered quite nice-looking," she said.

"Wow, that's probably a big compliment in your circle, isn't it?" I teased, thinking about the vanity of putting a flower in her hair.

She patted my arm. "You're learning."

"So, what did you want to be when you were a little kid?" I asked, making conversation. It was what adults always asked kids. I figured I'd turn it around.

But there was no answer. Unusual for her. I looked down at her snowy hair. "Aunt Frieda?"

"Oh, I was just thinking." She sounded puzzled. "I don't know if I ever thought about that, Ben. What I would be …"

"It's okay. Dumb question."

"No it's not. I suppose I knew I would marry and have children. But I did have questions about who I was. I remember once, when I was very young — oh, I told you about this, didn't I? When the workers arrived to help with the harvest?"

I nodded. "The music and the dancing."

"Yes. The Russian workers always did things differently. I thought they were quite romantic, the way they dressed and spoke. On the night I crept down to the orchards, I couldn't keep my eyes off that young couple. They were so free with their feelings ... I suppose that's what I heard in their music, even though I couldn't understand the words. It was as though it had touched their very souls."

We walked along the sidewalk. I found myself avoiding the cracks the way I did when I was a little kid, thinking about that young couple.

"Do you believe in God, Ben?'

Okay, major turnaround. "Huh?"

"God," she repeated quite loudly.

"Yeah, I heard you. Where'd that come from?"

"I'm old," she said, as if this were explanation enough. "Well?"

"I guess, yeah, probably ... in theory, anyway." I'd never given it much thought but sometimes — when I looked, say, at a tree or a really great-looking girl — I figured, yeah, probably.

"Well, I thought that night as I listened to the beautiful music that God must be listening as well ... but differently, because he would understand their language."

I tried to follow her.

She looked up at me. "You see, he didn't only understand our German language, he understood a thousand languages." Her eyes searched mine before she continued. "I'd always thought that the Mennonite people were special somehow, chosen by God. But that night under those bright stars, I knew He was much bigger than I'd ever thought. And I was happy to know this."

I could see the church a block away. I slowed my pace.

"But what about the bad stuff?" It probably wasn't fair to her, but it was what I thought about sometimes. Where was God when the music stopped?

"Oh, I was angry with God for a long time, Ben. Very angry. After Henry was taken, I prayed every night that God would deliver him back to me. I thought if only I had enough faith ... My family wrote to me from Canada reminding me that God would be my refuge and strength. And for a time these words and my prayers kept me warm at night. But time wore on, and I had no idea where they had taken him. I prayed, but there was no answer. I felt no refuge in God, and my heart began to freeze. I had my son and I loved him, but I felt so alone. We were very poor, and we lived in ... squalor. Every night Jacob would cry himself to sleep because of the lice ..."

Lice? My eyes widened. "Keep going."

"He was so uncomfortable and hungry — and I could do nothing for him. The letters from my family urged me to hold on to my faith, that good things would happen to those who wait. But I was so tired of waiting, Ben."

It was when she stopped talking that I noticed the traffic was moving quickly beside us. I felt as if it should have been horses and mud roads, prisons and soldiers.

"Then one day I received word from friends that Henry had been located, and he was being transferred to a prison not far from where we lived."

"So you got to see him?" I could actually feel my heart pumping blood.

"You're as impatient as I was." A faint flicker of a smile danced on her face, but then it vanished. "I left Jacob with friends, and I walked to the place where Henry was being held. It took me two days. I went to the man in charge and I asked to see my husband. He told me it was impossible. Impossible. I cried that whole night, and in the morning I returned to the prison, but the warden would not see me. I had failed — myself and Jacob. You see, I'd brought a photo to show Henry his son — ten years old. I walked beside the prison wall. There were men, soldiers, posted at every corner with their rifles."

"The men of stone."

She nodded. "At one end there was a fence, and through it I could see the courtyard. As I passed, prisoners were being led into the yard for the midday sun. I took hold of the fence and pressed my face to it, hoping to get a glimpse of my Henry. Then I saw —"

"Henry? You saw him?"

Aunt Frieda shook her head. "A guard. He was my age, perhaps younger. He walked toward me, his face stern and angry, his rifle pointed in my direction."

"I thought, at first, he was going to shoot me. I pulled myself tall, and God forgive me, I wanted him to pull the trigger. We looked at each other for a long time. But then his eyes changed. It was as though a veil was lifted. He jerked his head toward the prisoners. He walked away. I knew he was allowing me to look." Her face transformed as she smiled. "And that's when I saw Henry."

My fingernails dug into my palms, but I couldn't seem to unclench my fists.

Her voice was a whisper. "He was thinner and the hair that was left was almost gray. But I saw him ... our eyes met, and in that look was ten years of love I had missed. We couldn't speak, but that didn't matter. I'd seen him. I could touch him with my eyes." She grew teary. "And it was sufficient."

"It was sufficient," I repeated. "So what about the nightmares you have?"

She seemed jarred by my question. "The nightmares? How did you ..."

I hesitated. "Sometimes, at night, you have nightmares about lice, Aunt Frieda."

She shook her head sadly. "*Ach*, those nightmares. No, they had not even begun. When I returned home, I found that Jacob was gone. There had been trouble in the village, and families were forced to flee. My son was gone."

"Gone? Where? Who took him?"

"I heard he had left with the Rempel family. They were good people, but I had lost him. After my grief came anger. I was angry at God. I turned my back on Him, and I was alone. But Ben, no one can survive being that alone."

By now we'd arrived at the church, and people were milling around, smiling and shaking hands. I suddenly felt out of place in my running clothes.

"You won't come in?" Aunt Frieda asked.

"I'm gonna go for a run ... over there at the track." I pointed across the street. "I'll walk home with you, if you like."

"That will be fine," she said with a nod. "I'll see you in an hour."

I watched until she was inside the building, then I crossed the street and made my way to the track.

"No one can survive being that alone," she had said. But I had. Even though I had Mom and my sisters.

I had just started kindergarten when Dad had the accident. Mom had come home from the hospital alone. The girls had screamed, shouted, "No!" I covered my ears and ran to my room, hid in the closet and waited for my dad to tell me that my sisters were teasing me again. Finally Mom coaxed me out and held me. "He's not coming home" was all she'd said.

I hated this memory, hated that it had blocked out all the other memories I must have of my father. I picked up my pace and kept running, three, four, five times around the track, and then I lost count. Pretty soon the ache in my chest was replaced by my lungs pulling for air. But I just ran faster.

I'd been alone since that day but I had survived, hadn't I? Frieda was wrong.

When I couldn't run any more, I collapsed on a bench and listened to the blood thumping in my ears.

By the time I was breathing normally again, people were pouring out of church — nicely dressed people who didn't look as if they had any problems. But then, Stan looked normal on the outside. So did I. Even Claude the Demented looked sort of normal.

I crossed the street and waited in the shade of a cherry tree for Aunt Frieda. As soon as she emerged from the building, I waved, and she made her way through the crowd.

"So, how was it?" I asked.

"Very nice. The music was a bit loud — guitars and drums nowadays. But there were one or two hymns I recognized."

Her face looked rested.

"Such a young pastor," she continued, as we moved up the sidewalk. "He preached a good sermon, though, even if he couldn't have been more than forty!"

"Just a baby."

She cuffed me lightly on the head. "Rascal."

"Can I ask you something?" I said after a bit.

"Of course."

"How did you do it? How did you ... stand it when you came home — that day — and he, Jacob ..." Suddenly I wanted to pull back the question, but she didn't flinch.

"Where we lived, Jacob and I, there were terrible lice. It didn't matter what we did ... we washed, scrubbed with kerosene, even burned some of our things, but they kept coming back. Many nights Jake would cry himself to sleep from the pain of the bites, but there was nothing I could do except hold him."

My scalp actually felt itchy, but I resisted the urge to scratch.

"Once he was gone, what I held on to was the hope that where he was, there were no lice — and someone to hold him."

I felt my eyes prickle and I blinked hard. I hoped she hadn't noticed.

She didn't look at me, but she took my arm. I could feel the weight of her, slight as it was, pulling as though she needed the support. "Years later, when he was grown and sent for me, he told me that the day they had left the village, the lice disappeared." She smiled up at me, and in the sunlight, I could see that the lines on her face had been made as much by laughter as by sadness.

12

Later that afternoon, I phoned Stan to find out why I hadn't heard from him. His mom answered.

"He's not here."

"But I spoke to him yesterday. He said he was going to call you."

"He did. But he isn't coming home." And the line went dead.

All night I tried to figure out what could have gone wrong. One reason, he'd said, was all he needed. And I'd given him one.

～ ～ ～

The next morning I met up with Fish at the school gates, but it felt different.

"He sounded like he was coming back, right?" Fish asked.

"Something must have happened after I talked to him."

"You should've traced the call," he said.

I punched him on the arm, which hurt me, I'm sure, more than him. "Yeah, I shoulda pulled out my handy-dandy junior detective kit and put a trace on the call."

"Okay, okay." He rubbed his arm.

Inside the school, everything looked normal, which really pissed me off. Didn't people know everything had changed? Did anybody care that Stan was gone? Would anyone even notice?

Melody fluttered up to Fish at our lockers. I noticed Kat behind her, but I kept my face inside my locker to avoid saying something stupid.

Soon Fish had been pulled into Melody's orbit and was floating down the hall behind her. It was safe to turn, I figured, but when I did, Kat was standing directly in front of me.

"Whoa," I said, backing up a step and finding myself smushed against the metal bank of lockers.

She smiled and moved back — to give me room, I guessed.

"Hey," I said. Brilliant. My heart was racing and I wondered if she could tell, with those superhuman powers girls seemed to have.

"I heard your obnoxious friend skipped town."

In a millisecond, she went from being Supergirl to utterly ordinary. Even my heartbeat slowed.

"He's not obnoxious." I moved past her toward my class.

I could hear her behind me, and then she touched my arm. Her cheeks were tinged pink.

"I'm sorry," she said. "That was dumb. Really dumb." She seemed sincere ... and my heart went at it again. It was like a lawnmower motor — one pull and off it went.

"Are you worried about him? Melody says he's been gone for a couple of days."

I moved to the side of the hallway, out of the human current.

"I thought he was coming back last night," I said. "That's what he told me, but I don't know. Maybe he's off on a road trip — California, Mexico —"

"But you don't think so?"

I shook my head. "I don't think so."

"Well, I hope he's okay." Then she reached out and touched my arm again, and it felt like a branding iron, only cool. So cool that when she took it away, I could still feel the imprint.

She started toward the throng of students but then stopped. She pulled at a strand of her hair. "So, uh, why didn't you ask me to dance the other night?" Now her cheeks were quite red — and quite, quite beautiful.

I shifted from my right foot to the left. I mentally calculated possible answers quickly: I had to leave. Lame. I needed to look for Stan. Lamer and, additionally, not true. "But I wanted to ask," I said finally.

She tucked the strand of hair behind a perfect ear. "You could have," she said. And then the bell rang, and she walked away.

I watched her until she disappeared into a classroom. The halls were getting less crowded. I was going to be late for history, and with my record of skipping classes, I couldn't afford that. I decided to take a shortcut through the courtyard, an area partly obscured by large cedar trees. I walked quickly, but I soon realized that I wasn't alone. I looked behind me. Claude, Jeff and Arnie had followed me. I hurried, but Claude stepped around and into my path. Behind me, I could hear his friends breathing.

I tried to sidestep Claude, pretending that he wasn't there, but he headed me off, placing his weight-trained bulk uncomfortably close.

"Guess you're not so brave without your bodyguards around, eh?" he said.

"Actually, Claude, I'm not that brave even when they are around," I said, looking straight at him. "But then, I don't see you walking around on your own much either."

This was probably not the greatest idea I'd ever had in my life, but I was suddenly tired of wondering when he was going to strike again.

He pushed me, and I stumbled backward but didn't fall.

"I saw you talking to Kat." He pushed again. "She's way out of your league, Ballerina Boy. I don't want to see it again." He stood, poised to push again, laughing over my shoulder at his guffawing buddies — like I was such a no-threat I'd wait patiently for the next blow. I was instantly furious; I could actually feel the adrenaline pouring through my body. Aunt Frieda's warden ... and the men who'd taken Henry away — all of them must have looked just like Claude. I pushed hard on his chest. Taken by surprise, he fell to the ground. Before I could do anything, somebody pinned my arms behind me.

The first hit landed on my nose, and as the pain exploded inside my head, I could actually feel the bone and cartilage crumple. The blows kept coming — my left cheek, the side of my head, my shoulder. I could hear myself grunting as the air was being pushed out of my lungs, but at the same time I was watching it — this thing — happen to me. It didn't seem real. This happened on television, in the movies — in history books. Not to me. Because it wasn't just my body being pummeled; with each hit Claude was trying to get his hands on something deep inside me, something just out of reach. And I knew I was hanging on. My eyes were closed, but I could see colors zigzagging against the inside of my eyelids. And then black.

I woke up with Nurse Shapiro peering down at me. I shifted my head in the direction of slow-motion voices. Shepherd and the principal, Ms. Sterne, were standing in the corner of the nurse's office.

"He's awake," Nurse Shapiro said over her shoulder.

I tried to raise myself on one elbow, but my arm wouldn't cooperate. I fell back against the pillow.

"Don't try to move. The ambulance is on its way."

"Who did this to you?" Ms. Sterne's sharp nose was directly above me. Even in the pain, I wondered if she'd ever considered investing in a good pair of tweezers.

"Could I have some water?" I asked.

"I don't think that's a good idea. At least not right now," clucked the nurse.

"Was it Claude?" Shepherd's face came into view, and I felt I was going to suffocate. I wanted to punch the faces out of my way. I couldn't breathe.

"Give him some room. Please." Nurse Shapiro's decisive bark sent them both scuttling to the side of the room. Gratefully, I drew in some air.

Then something in the corner of the room caught my eye, something pink and torn and ruffly. I tried to focus, but it was the sudden recognition in Shepherd's eyes, and the way he looked, that made me feel sick to my stomach.

"What's that?" I asked. My voice sounded like sandpaper.

"Nothing, Ben. At least not now."

But Ms. Sterne picked it up and brought it over. Her voice was kind. "We found this around your feet, Ben. Please, you have to help us punish whoever did this to you."

I looked at the pink crinoline — somebody's idea of a tutu. My head boomed. I felt such hatred burst inside me that I realized I'd never understood the word until now.

The ambulance guys poked and prodded, lifting limbs and pressing to see where I was damaged. I tried to float away. What a disappointment my body was — so bloody fragile. I couldn't help thinking how invincible I felt when I was dancing. How every part of me responded to my orders — even as I ached with exhaustion. Now everything was spinning out of control, beyond my reach. I closed my eyes, willed the blackness to come.

I refused to open my eyes until I was in a hospital bed in the emergency room and some of the bodies had retreated. Someone was holding my wrist, so I slowly opened my right eye — the left one was glued shut. A butt-ugly doctor grimaced down at me.

"I'm Dr. Balch," he bellowed, as if my hearing had been affected.

"I was hoping for a beautiful blonde just out of medical school."

"Only on television, I'm afraid," he chuckled. "I'm glad your sense of humor wasn't damaged."

"Who's joking?" I grumbled, trying to sit up. My shoulder burned with pain.

"You'll want to be careful with that shoulder, Ben. It was partially dislocated. Other than that, there's some bruises and swelling, but that's it. You're pretty lucky."

"Right. I was just thinking that same thing." I saw his nose twitch, as if he was tiring of my wit.

"The police are here," he said. "They want to ask you a few questions."

A uniform entered the room, pulled a chair up and sat beside the bed.

"Hello, son."

I mumbled hello, even though it is my least favorite thing when total strangers call me "son."

"I won't take too much time. You look as if you could use a little rest."

"That's why I checked in, for a rest." He looked as unimpressed as the doctor had.

"Son, did you see who did this to you?"

"My name's Ben."

He didn't seem to hear, just waited for my answer. In the blink of that moment, I made a decision. No one, not even the police, was going to take this away from me. I shook my head. "They came at me from behind. It was over too quick."

"They?"

"It, uh, yeah."

"They didn't take anything — that's what your teacher said. He mentioned a boy at school who he thought might —"

"I didn't see anything."

"A voice? Did they say anything?"

I shook my head. "Random act of violence," I offered.

The officer scribbled something in his notebook, and I thought he sighed. "Yup ... see a lot of that." He stopped writing. "I also see a lot of kids who take on things best left to the police." He gave me a look dripping with meaning.

I nodded as if he was talking about somebody else.

"Here's my card. Call me if you remember anything, s—, er, Ben." He placed the white business card beside the neon-green jello on my tray.

"Yup."

As soon as he left the room, Dr. Balch stepped forward. "Your mother should be here soon."

Mom? I groaned. Blood and guts were not her thing. And hospitals? She hated them ... hadn't stepped inside one since —

"Ben, oh Ben." She walked through the doors slowly, looking around like she was on the set of a horror movie. "Are you all right?" She stepped forward and hugged me carefully.

"Ow!" I yelped, and she sprang back.

"His shoulder will be pretty sore," Dr. Balch explained.

"How did this happen? Who would do such a thing to you?"

It was on the tip of my tongue to tell her about Claude, but something held me back. It wasn't fear, it was something completely new to me — revenge. Comic-book, science-fiction, movie-theater-with-popcorn, Hollywood revenge. I wanted it really badly, and I wanted to get it myself. Seeing Claude punished would not be enough. My whole body tingled with the thought of crushing his face.

"I didn't see them coming. Someone grabbed my arms — they jumped me," I answered, going for partial truths.

"Maybe you'll remember more after a while, honey. You're probably still in shock." She turned to the doctor. "Can he come home with me now?"

Dr. Balch shook his head. "I don't think he has a concussion, but I don't want to take any chances. He can go home tomorrow."

Mom looked ready to crawl out of her skin, and I hated Claude even more for what this was doing to her. I found a phony, cheerful voice. "I'll be okay, Mom. It's not that bad. Honest."

"I'll stay with you."

"Mom, it's okay." The last thing she could take was a night in a hospital. "I'm going to sleep as soon as you leave. I'm a big boy, okay? Besides, don't you have a class to teach?"

She spent the next half hour plumping pillows, arranging for a television set, buying magazines and chocolate bars. She looked about to talk a couple of times, but then she'd just do something to keep herself busy.

Finally, she was ready to leave, and I was relieved to see her go.

"The girls will want to visit tonight," she said at the door.

"No, Mom. Not the girls." That was the last thing I needed. Mad alone could weep and wail loud enough to wake the dead, or at least the comatose. Joni would be painting pain for a month straight, and who knew what cooking tail-spin this would send Beth into — muffins molded into fists, pasta shaped like swollen lips? "Please, Mom, promise me!"

"Okay, okay. You're probably right. They are a little emotional sometimes."

The first smile of the day reached my puffy lips. "Just a little."

She left, and I promptly dozed off from the painkillers. When I woke up, feeling blurry around the edges, the first thing I saw was Fish's big face at the foot of my bed. He looked pissed off.

"Claude?"

"Fine, thanks, how are you?"

"Yeah, yeah ... you look like crap. It was Claude, wasn't it?"

I nodded.

Fish jumped to his feet and turned in a circle, clenching his fists. "I'm going to get him — don't worry about it."

"No you're not."

"You're going to let him get away with this?"

I shook my head. "I want you to do something for me but not that."

He sat down. "What, then?"

"I want you to teach me how to fight."

13

A slow smile curved across Fish's face. "I can do that, but you aren't exactly in condition."

"He won't bother me right away — he's too smart for that. He'll lie low for a while, till he realizes I haven't ratted on him."

"We can go to my gym. Use the ring there."

I nodded. "Have you heard anything from Stan?"

"Nah. Nobody has. I tried calling his house, but his dad didn't know anything. The police are looking for him."

"He can't run forever, though, right? He'll be back," I said with more conviction than I felt. Deep down, I wondered if we'd ever see him again.

We watched some television, and then Fish left. I kept the tube on for company, but I couldn't concentrate. I couldn't see anything except the picture in my head of Claude, crumpled and bloody, at my feet.

~ ~ ~

I awoke early with an ancient nurse holding my wrist. Before my vision cleared I thought it was Aunt Frieda.

"You'll be able to go home today, young man. How did you sleep?"

I'd had stupid dreams all night long. Claude's ugly mug, Stan floating in and out ... my sisters singing in a choir — that was a weird one — and through the entire thing, like a cheesy soundtrack, a chant. "Lice, lice, lice."

"Like a baby."

━ ～ ～

Mom picked me up at the hospital that afternoon. She drove home telling me stories about her students, mostly rambling on about nothing. I nodded once in a while to give the impression that I was listening.

"Where's the marching band?" I asked, after Beth insisted on seating me down on the La-Z-Boy recliner.

As I expected, the girls had used the "incident" as an event. There was a "Welcome Home" banner, chocolate cake, an armload of flowers (what fifteen-year-old boy wouldn't love that?) and lots of painful hugging.

It wasn't that I didn't appreciate the thought, but, "You guys are too much," I said. They beamed through teary eyes at me.

"Poor, poor Benjo, how could anyone hit —" said Beth.

"— such a cute face. What kind of creep —" added Mad.

"The world is full of creeps," Joni muttered.

"We're so glad you're not like that, Benny."
Beth again.

I forced my lips into a smile-like configuration.
"I'm going to my room for a while."

Beth and Mad sprang forward. "Let us help you."

I pushed their flailing hands away and could see
the hurt look on their identical faces.

Aunt Frieda looked small and concerned in the
corner. I couldn't meet her eyes.

As I left the room, Mom was explaining the effects
of traumatic injury. She was good at outlining the
facts, the hows. It was the whys she had trouble with.

Go ahead. Figure this one away, Mom.

I knew they'd chew this whole thing over for the
entire evening. They'd examine the "psycho-socio-
logical factors" and make it into some big cosmic
thing. (Not that they'd agree on what that thing
was.) But it was simple: Claude beat me up. I was
going to pay him back. Revenge. Finally beat up on
every bad thing ever done to me. Every guy who'd
ever razzed me about dancing. My sisters and my
mom, who didn't have a clue who I was. The men of
stone who'd hurt Aunt Frieda. Stan's parents for
being stupid and incompetent. So simple.

— ~ —

I talked Mom into letting me eat in my room that
night. Mad and Beth brought a tray to me. They
looked unusually small as they entered the room.

"Sorry about before, Benjo —"

"— too much all at once —"

"— must be tired and you need —"

I held up my hand like a crossing guard. "Could you ever, in your lives, talk one at a time? Finish one complete sentence?"

"Well, you don't have to be rude," huffed Mad, and she stormed from the room.

"She should really consider nursing if the acting thing doesn't work out."

Beth smiled as she put the tray down. "We're worried about you, Benny."

"Do you think you could just call me Ben?"

She reached out a hand, I think to ruffle my hair, but stopped herself. "Sure, of course. We're just used to you being the ... you know."

"Baby."

She smiled apologetically. "Look what I made," she said proudly, lifting the napkin. "Hamburgers!"

I smiled even though it hurt my split lip. "On a bed of greens," I added.

She shrugged. "I couldn't help myself. Bon appetit." She turned at the doorway. "Mom said you didn't see who beat you up."

I grunted.

Her eyes narrowed. "You're not going to do something stupid, are you?"

"Who, me? Sensible, sensitive me?"

"Benj ... Ben. Don't sink to their level. It's not safe."

"What do you want me to do, Beth? Just lie down and take it?"

"There are other ways … look at Jesus … look at Gandhi! Violence is for barbarians."

"Gandhi and Jesus? So, what, my options are assassination or crucifixion?"

Beth leaned against the door. "Enjoy your burger, Ben," she said in a tired voice and left.

I tried to eat my meal but I wasn't hungry. What did she want from me? What did any of them want from me? All my life they'd told me about the man I should never become: the know-it-all, the brute, the insensitive goof, the guy-who-never-listens. What about the man I *should* become? They'd never said anything about that.

— — —

Fish brought my homework by. I heard him clumping down the hallway, pretty much ruling out future employment as a spy. He came into the room carrying two plates piled high with chocolate cake and ice cream.

"Man, you live in heaven," he declared, handing me a plate. "And Beth? She's really cute. Why have I never noticed that before?"

"Maybe because you're supposed to be in love with Melody?"

"A guy can look, can't he?"

"Well, don't let Stan see you looking," I answered, forgetting for a second that Stan was gone. The room felt heavier immediately. "Why don't you focus on Joni?" I tried, but it didn't help.

Fish shook his head, his mouth full of chocolate cake. He swallowed. "Uh-uh, she scares me. She's so … ferocious, or something."

"Welcome to my world, buddy."

"Besides, there's something about a dame who can cook."

We spent the next thirty seconds demolishing the cake.

Fish shoved his plate under the chair before leaning on the back two legs, his size-twelve feet on my bed.

"You really look pretty bad," he said thoughtfully. "Kind of yellow and oozing."

"Thanks."

"Yellow and oozing," he repeated. "That sounds good. Stan would have liked that."

"We gotta stop talking like he's dead, Fish. We have to find him, do something."

"I know. But if the police can't find him, what chance do we have?"

Helpless. The word might as well have flashed across our chests like a subtitle in a foreign movie. I could see Aunt Frieda's face pressed against the fence, watching Henry trapped inside.

Claude.

Fighting back.

"Did you check out the gym?" I asked. "When can we start?"

"Buddy." Fish pulled his feet off the bed, leaned forward. "You look like a salmon that just swam upstream."

"You really are a poet, man. Forget how I look. I'm ready."

"Listen, I'm the first one to say Claude needs the crap kicked out of him, but give it a couple of days, okay?"

"Okay," I agreed reluctantly.

He dug into his knapsack and pulled out a notebook. He handed me a math sheet and an English assignment. "Shepherd stopped me in the hallway today."

I swallowed twice to keep my throat open. He wouldn't have told Fish about … the other thing, would he, what Claude and his creeps had put around my legs. "He's still on the warpath?" I managed to get out.

"I didn't tell him anything. He thought I would."

"He's hopeless." I relaxed just a little. Fish wouldn't be able to look me in the eye if he knew.

"He just wants to help, Ben."

"You don't think I should tell him?" My voice rose a notch.

"No way. Claude would be suspended for a couple

of days, get to look like the bad boy. Forget it. There's nothing they can do."

Good. It was official. It was up to me.

—◆— —◆— —◆—

I went to bed early that night, determined to get the sleep I needed to recover. Suddenly my whole life revolved around my revenge. Nothing else mattered — except for Stan, but somehow it all seemed connected. If I could get Claude, beat him down, erase him, Stan would come home and things would be better. Okay, it didn't make sense in any logical way, but it made sense to me.

—◆— —◆— —◆—

"Stop ... my hands ..." My hands were tied behind my back and ropes dug into my wrists. Blood was seeping around the rope, thickening and congealing. *"Stop."* My skin was crawling. Something was actually crawling under it, black and shiny. Hard. Alive. *"Lice."*

I tried to lift my head, open my eyes, but they stayed plastered shut ... swollen and full of pus. If I didn't wake up, I was going to die — the room was shrinking. And then something warm touched my hand and the ropes fell away. Something warm and dry and soft. A hush filled my brain and my eyelids separated.

Aunt Frieda was beside the bed. Her hand stroked mine gently. "Shh, *nah yo*. Rest, *mein bengel*."

My head fell back against the pillow and I slept.

In the morning there was no sign that Aunt Frieda had actually been there. But I could have sworn ...

I maneuvered my aching body out of bed and dressed for school. One more day of tender loving care and I'd be ready for the loony bin.

I looked into Aunt Frieda's room, but she was sound asleep.

When I entered the kitchen, Joni glanced up from the paper. Beth was posted at the stove, and Mad was pulling out of some impossible yoga position on the floor. They all seemed surprised to see me.

"Morning," I said, normal as could be. I tried not to wince as I sat down.

"Good morning, Master Ben. How nice to see you up and about this lovely morning," Mad said in clipped tones. She put a hand to her face. "My goodness, did I actually speak in a full and complete sentence?"

I grabbed a muffin from the basket. "Get over it."

Mad stretched her torso along her legs like a human paper clip.

"So you're 'the man' now, huh, Ben?" said Joni. "One thrashing and you're ... what, Robo-brother?"

I reached for part of the paper. "Shut up."

She walked out of the room.

"Where's Mom?" I asked Beth.

"Early class. She thought you'd be sleeping till noon. You're not going to school today, are you?"

"I'm fine."

"Like we care," Mad said, pulling herself into a standing position. She grabbed a muffin. "I've got rehearsal today, Beth. I won't be home for dinner."

"Good luck. Break a leg," Beth called after her.

I kept my head bent over the paper.

When I looked up again, Beth was sitting beside me. She reached out a hand and brushed her fingertips on my bruised face.

"Don't touch me." I lurched back like I'd been burned.

Her eyes filled with tears. "What did he do to you?"

When I didn't answer, she, too, left the room.

14

"… expecting great things from you people," Shepherd paused meaningfully.

He liked to call us "you people," as though we were somehow different, separate from the rest of the human race.

Max Ton's hand shot up. "I'm confused."

The class laughed, but Shepherd held up his hand to silence the sniggering. Max, as usual, was unperturbed.

"Go on," Shepherd said.

"I'm almost finished my research, Mr. Shepherd."

"Dork," somebody called out.

With one hand, Shepherd ushered whoever it was out the back door. I didn't even turn to see who it was.

"Proceed, Mr. Ton," Shepherd said smoothly.

"Well, I can't really figure out who's who. I mean, there's the Red Army and the White Army … the

Czarists — what are they, the Monarchists? The Bolsheviks, the Communists, the Fascists — who can keep them all straight?"

"And your question is?" Shepherd asked patiently.

"It all keeps changing. How do you know who the bad guys are?"

"Why do there have to be bad guys?"

Max had no ready answer.

"Makes it easier to shoot them," I said, surprising myself more than anyone else.

Shepherd pushed his half glasses up on his nose as if he wanted to read me. "Tell me there's some irony in your voice, Mr. Conrad."

I shrugged, sorry I'd spoken. My swollen eye was pulling with tiredness, and I just wanted to sleep. "Sure."

Shepherd stuck his glasses into his shirt pocket. He had his hopeful-teacher look stretched across his face. "No, really, Mr. Conrad. Elaborate. Why does it make it easier to shoot them? To what end?"

"To the end of them. They're gone, erased. Then they can't hurt anybody," I said, muffled and quiet, but he was listening.

"And how do we recognize the bad guys?" His teacher voice was gone. He was just a person now.

"It's in the eyes," I said.

He didn't say anything — for the first time. And the strange thing was, part of me wanted him to have a really great, smart response. Prove me wrong, I wanted to shout. Give me one good reason —

But the bell rang. I picked up my books and filed out of the room with everyone else.

Two days later I found myself at the gym with Fish. The room pulsed like it was a living, sweating organism. Every inch of space was occupied with guys pumping iron. In the center of the room was a ring marked by rope, a neat, organized square for civilized, organized fighting.

One of the trainers, Alec, fitted us with gloves. He had a medium build and wasn't much taller than me, but he looked strong and fit. He taught us the basics.

"Boxing is an athletic contest between two people," he started in a low, soft voice. "You use your fists to try to knock the other unconscious or to inflict enough punishment to cause your opponent to quit or be judged defeated ..."

Fish nodded knowingly. He'd had a couple of lessons last year. But I sucked it all in like a baby taking in my first lungful of true air. "Knock the other unconscious." Sounded good to me.

Claude had been suspiciously absent for the past few days, but he was always with me.

"Maybe he knows he went too far," Fish had said.

"He's biding his time."

"Sounds like something Stan would say."

Stan. He was with us too. The longer he stayed away, the more he was with us.

Alec was still talking — something about ancient Rome when they'd maimed or killed an opponent. "Remember, though, the emphasis in boxing is not on strength as much as agility. It's not about beating your opponent as much as it is about pushing through your own pain. Pushing yourself to the limit, that's the point."

I didn't know much about the pushing through pain part, but I understood agility. This was encouraging.

I pulled the strings on the gloves tight with my teeth. It felt weird wearing these big, bulbous leather extensions of clenched fists. Almost cowardly.

Alec left us in the ring. We had on helmets as well as mouth guards. Protection he called it.

Fish stood calmly as I came out swinging.

"Control," he said. "Wait for the moment."

He moved around me, hunched over, protecting vital organs. His arms were up, his fists ready. I watched him from the center, then I began to copy his moves, circling around him. It was a dance. He didn't know it, I was sure of that. But it was definitely a dance. My legs felt less heavy, and I could hear music in my head — only a beat, but music. I moved in three quick dance steps without thinking, a *pas de bourrée*, to be precise, not that I'd ever tell Fish.

"That's good. That's right. You're getting it."

My arm, as if spring loaded, darted out, catching Fish lightly on the chin strap. He hadn't seen it coming.

"Okay, smart boy." Fish grinned. His right hand caught me neatly on the side of my helmet, but I spun away from him. That was easy, familiar. I moved back to miss his left hook — and then forward to connect right under his chin. He was surprised and stopped moving, just watching me as I came at him again. I stopped in my tracks.

"What?"

"You're a natural," he said quietly. There was admiration in his eyes — I'd never seen that before.

~ ~ ~

After each session at the gym, I felt more alive and in control. My shoulder was nearly back to normal and the bruises were fading. I was almost my old self. Except I wasn't. What happened in the courtyard with Claude had changed me. I would never again be someone's target.

We still hadn't heard from Stan. The last time I called his mother, I'd heard desperation in her voice. Tough, I thought. Much too little and far too late.

One evening as I was practicing jabs in the mirror, Aunt Frieda walked by. I should have closed my door.

"Who's winning?" she asked, smiling.

I grinned sheepishly. "It's a draw, I think."

"May I sit down?"

"Sure." I pulled my desk chair out for her.

"I haven't seen you very much lately. I've missed our talks," she said.

I shrugged. "I've been busy with school stuff." It was amazing how easy lying was becoming.

"I think your sisters miss you as well."

I laughed out loud at that. "Uh-uh. No way."

"What makes you so sure?"

"That's just the way it is around here, Aunt Frieda. There's me and there's them. It's always been that way." Not quite true either. I had a feeling — and a few photos to back this up — that me and my dad used to do guy things together. Tossing a baseball. Kicking a soccer ball at the park. I used to be part of an "us."

"It works out okay, Aunt Frieda. I give them their space, they give me mine."

Her eyes looked sad. "You're planning to fight this boy then? This boy who gave you the black eye?"

Caught by a left hook out of nowhere. "I'm, uh, just training. You know, getting in shape. It's dangerous out there," I said noncommittally.

"There are other ways of fighting back, Ben."

"Beth said the same thing," I said, sitting down on my bed. "Tell me honestly — when they took Henry away or when Jacob left ... didn't you want to fight back, Aunt Frieda?" I leaned over, my elbows on my knees. Maybe it was unfair — I shouldn't upset her — but I really wanted to know.

"Of course, Ben. Every night after Henry was taken, I thought about revenge. I was filled with rage. 'All things work for good,' people told me. Pah. These words meant nothing. My thoughts of revenge kept me warm, kept me company — they were all I had left."

"So what did you do?" I thought of that rush of heat when I imagined smashing Claude's face with my fist, feeling and hearing the bones give way.

"All my life I'd been told how wrong it was to fight: if you reached for the sword, you would die by the sword. But this too meant nothing. The men of stone had taken what was precious from me. Didn't they deserve to suffer? Night after night I imagined ways to make them hurt. I concocted such tortures in my mind that they would beg for mercy. My mercy."

As she spoke, a light burned in her eyes that made me uneasy. I couldn't imagine that an old lady could own such feelings. It didn't fit with the loving way she acted with my family. I couldn't look any more. I put my head in my hands.

Gradually I heard a softer voice. "Then I dreamed, Ben, but not my usual nightmare. I dreamed that I was standing outside the prison, waiting. Then the fence — the chains — fell away. And I was in the middle of the courtyard. I was walking toward Henry. He was standing in the sunlight. I reached out to him, but when he turned, it wasn't Henry I touched. It was the guard, the man who'd let me see Henry. His eyes were kind. He was not my enemy. He was only a man, and all he could do was shoot me. My true enemy was the hatred inside me, and it could do far more harm."

"I don't understand that."

"I was exhausted, Ben. Hatred is an all-consuming master. So much had been taken from me. The only thing I had left was my humanity. I couldn't let the men of stone take that as well."

I shook my head, not understanding — not wanting to understand.

"When you dance, Ben, do you always know where the music will lead you?"

Her words jarred me into the present. What did she know about dance? Nothing. Claude or me. It wasn't about my humanity, it was about survival.

When I looked up, she had left.

～ ～ ～

After that, I avoided my family even more. It was easy with Joni and Mad because they were ignoring me, as if the silent treatment would be too unbearable and I'd come crawling. Mom tried to figure out where I "was at," but Psych 100 wasn't enough, and she gave up as long as I was home by curfew. Beth just looked sad, which tore me up, but I told myself that things would get back to normal once I'd had it out with Claude. Everything would be better and Stan would come back.

I avoided Aunt Frieda as well. She seemed to want something from me that I couldn't give. At nights I felt she sat at my bedside, but I was never sure. And when morning came, there was no sign.

After school, I'd go straight to the gym. Sometimes Fish came with me, but most often I'd go alone. I burned inside like a chemical fire, sucking everything living out of the air. I was pumping iron as well as sparring, building muscles and getting stronger. I liked the feeling of power it gave me — to push harder, to feel the tendons and muscles pulling and straining until I thought they'd pop. Sometimes Alec would give me a few tips, mumble about moving through the pain ... and tell me to take it easy. But I wouldn't take it easy. I was possessed.

Besides, it helped me to not think about Stan, lost and wandering around out there.

The other day, Fish and I had stopped by to see if there was any news. Eventually Mrs. Belado answered the bell, looking cross and beaten down.

"He's not here," she said through the screen door. She turned, responding to someone inside.

"Shut up, I can't hear myself think."

Mr. Belado came up the sidewalk behind us. He just sidestepped and walked through the doorway without a glance or a word to his wife.

"Nice of you to drop by," she muttered as he slid past. "There's no news," she said to us, but this time her eyes looked sad, and I felt a pang of pity.

"He'll come home," I said.

She looked at me, her eyelids half closed, as if it took too much effort to open them wide. "He's always been trouble, that one. I keep a roof over his head, feed him. Nothing's ever enough."

Fish was already backing away at this point, embarrassed and tugging at my arm. But I couldn't leave. I wanted to say something to her, something about how Stan had always stood up for me, always been there for me. How he made me feel good about myself. But I couldn't find the words, and she just shrugged and closed the door in my face.

I tried to imagine her on the other side of the door, caring — but I couldn't.

I picked up the weights now and hoisted them up to my chest. I felt my biceps tremble with exertion and watched the veins pull just under my skin. My face was blank — I was getting good at that. It was completely different from dance, where facial expression is as important as movement. But in this place you kept it to yourself —

the pain, the triumph — and let your body tell the story.

By the time I got home most nights, I was too tired to do anything except eat and go to bed.

Aunt Frieda was always in the kitchen, often with one of the girls. I knew Beth was interested in learning some of her recipes, and sometimes I'd hear Aunt Frieda's instructions — kneading, rolling dough, deep frying.

"Come try this, *mein bengel*," she said now, handing me a bowl of stew. "We need a man's opinion here."

"You need a man's opinion? That's a first around here," I said, but I took the bowl and scarfed it down.

She smiled as she watched. I smiled back as I handed her the bowl. "It was okay." I shrugged, and she ruffled my hair with her small hand. For a second, her warmth almost went through me. Even Joni seemed softer when Aunt Frieda was around. But I couldn't let that happen to me. I needed my edge ... to be on my guard. I needed to be ready.

I backed away. "I'm going to my room."

The next day Fish didn't show up at the gym. But Alec said he'd fight me. As I got ready, I felt my muscles tighten with expectation, almost the way I felt before a performance. Almost. But there was no music in my head.

Someone clanged the bell, and we circled, bodies hunched, guarded against a blow, looking into each other's eyes.

He threw the first punch. I raised my glove swiftly and deflected the blow.

I jabbed once, twice ... faking. The third jab landed on the side of Alec's face. He smiled even as his head jerked to the side.

"Good hit," he said, approvingly.

I didn't smile back. "Ballerina Boy" bounced around in my head like a Ping-Pong ball.

We circled some more. The pulse in my ears provided the beat, steadily increasing as we exchanged blows. But the refrain grew louder and louder — "Ballerina Boy" — and Alex became Claude. And then, for the briefest second, it seemed as if my father was there, standing outside the ring. I blinked the sweat out of my eyes and the image was gone. I was disoriented, lost.

Alec's fist grazed my chin, and suddenly I was furious — enraged — and nothing mattered except bringing Claude down. My fists connected — with his head, his chin, his chest, his kidneys — and then arms were pulling me away. Claude — no, Alec — was on the floor of the ring, doubled over and groaning.

I bent over, sucking in air. I'd won. It was war and I had won.

But that's not what they said when they told me to go home. They called my punches illegal and told me to get the hell out. I apologized to Alec, told him I hadn't meant to go so far.

But he didn't make it any easier. "You're missing the point here, Ben."

As I walked home, I waited for the anger to subside, waited for my old self to come back. But it didn't.

I was missing the point? Damn right I was. What was the point? Nobody was brave enough, honest enough to admit that there wasn't one. People like my dad died in stupid car accidents. Men like Henry were torn from their beds and taken away. Kids like Stan and Jacob disappeared, and nobody would just come out and say that it made no sense.

A car drove fast through a puddle, and I could feel the mud splash up onto my clothes. I heard a laugh — maybe from the disappearing car, I couldn't tell. But it filled me with white-hot rage — like in the ring but even more intense — and it felt good because it felt like something. My fist closed around a rock. It was jagged and cut into my skin. The next thing I knew I was throwing it — and then another and another. I could hear glass shatter. It felt as if my head was going to split open. Then there was nothing. Nothing at all until I felt my arms pinned behind my back.

The back seat of a police car is not as clean as you might expect. There were chocolate bar wrappers and coffee cups, and it smelled of somebody who'd never given deodorant a passing thought.

Officer Ray had wrapped my hand in a bandage, and decided to take me home instead of the local juvy lockup. I wasn't sure that a night in jail wouldn't have been easier than facing my mother. I could see the look of disbelief on her face as she opened the door to him. I could imagine her saying, You must be mistaken. My son would never damage public property. My sisters would form a chorus. Not Benny. Not our little brother.

But then Officer Ray returned to the car and deposited me, still handcuffed, on the front stoop. Every mother's dream.

Her face lost all color, and for the first time I felt sick. And sick I was, all over the rose bush. Officer Ray took pity on me then and removed the handcuffs. Beth led me to the couch.

It was Aunt Frieda I couldn't look at. It's a cliché, I know, but I wanted the ground to open up and swallow me.

Beth was clucking, Mad was questioning and Joni was scowling when Mom told them all to leave. Aunt Frieda followed them out the door.

Mom stared, then paced. Finally she sat down on the couch beside me. I could smell my own vomit and said I wanted to go clean up. I got halfway off the couch.

"No."

I sat down again.

"The gym called, so I've been filled in on your crazed behavior there. Maybe you could pick it up after that." Sarcasm dripped from her voice. An interesting choice, I thought.

"I, uh, broke some windows, I think."

"You broke some windows, you t*hink*?"

"The cop said it was an abandoned building, Mom."

"Well, that's okay then. What's all the fuss about? Can I get you something to eat?" Her voice was frigid.

I considered a joke about ordering in pizza but reconsidered.

"I'm fine," I said instead.

For the next I don't know how long, she paced, until I was ready to scream.

"Say something," I finally said.

"I don't know what to say." Her voice was shaking now. "There could have been people inside that building ... you could have seriously injured that man at the gym. My God, do you realize what you've done!"

It suddenly hit me — she hadn't asked me why. She wanted an explanation, something that might make sense of it. But did she want to know why? And I think I even wanted to tell her — at least as much as I was able because I wasn't totally sure myself. But I could see from the look on her face that she didn't want to know. It horrified me and felt familiar at the same time.

"I'm sorry," I said instead. Sorry she didn't want to know.

"We're both upset, Ben. It's late. Let's finish this in the morning."

I took a long shower that night. I scrubbed until the dried blood disappeared from the inside of my hand and the smell of puke had faded away.

I dreaded the knock on my door, but I knew it would come. And it did.

"May I come in?" Aunt Frieda asked.

"Um, no." I said weakly.

The door opened. "I know you're tired, *mein bengel*. I'll only be a moment." She sat at the foot of my bed. "How is your hand?"

"Fine. I'm just really tired."

"I know. Too tired for a boy your age."

"I'm not a boy."

"Yes you are," she said firmly. "And I want to tell you about another boy."

I covered my face with my good hand. "Please, no more stories." I thought this would shut her up, but she actually laughed.

"Oh, phht, I have a thousand stories. I'll tell you each and every one of them if you don't be quiet and listen."

I took the hand away from my face, but I didn't smile.

"When your father was about your age, maybe a little older, he stopped coming to church," she began. "His parents — my brother — were worried about this, afraid for his soul, Ben. They asked me to talk to him because they knew that Neil liked to talk to me. Also I am a very big busybody, as you know."

No other story would have interested me now — my hand was throbbing and my head felt like a twenty-pound bowling ball. But she caught me. My father caught me.

"So did he? Talk to you?"

"Oh yes. He told me that he was being suffocated by our ways. Has your mother told you why he visited home so seldom?"

"Sure. She's very chatty on the subject of my father."

She ignored me. "Your father was an artist, Ben. He saw the world differently ... as light and shapes and vibrant colors. Our people's idea of beauty was order and symmetry and ... black and white. His parents didn't see an artist's life as either practical or orderly. How would he provide for a family?"

"What has this —"

"Phht," she silenced me. Obviously I was pissing the old lady off.

"Neil wasn't understood by his own, Ben. He was deeply uncomfortable in his own culture, and he refused to be limited by it. For me, I have been deeply comforted by the Mennonite ways — there is a richness there and a safety that I feel deeply in my soul. But this wasn't the case for your father. So he had to leave in order to save himself."

I struggled to understand. "Are you saying that I should leave?"

"*Nein, nein,* of course not. What I'm saying is that you must choose what defines who you are. The truth of who one is is complex — it is not merely good or simply bad. I believe that truth is the image of God in which we were created, but it has taken me a lifetime of experiences and choices to discover this. You have to find your own way. Don't let yourself be limited by the hatred you feel. Don't let it stop your search."

"Huh."

"What is this, huh?"

"My mom always says that people only have themselves. That's a big deal with her, self-reliance."

"Your mother has had to handle a lot on her own."

"So did you, but you didn't let yourself die inside."

The words shocked both of us — but she just sort of nodded. Man, living through a couple of wars gave her a thick skin.

"Your mother and father were deeply in love. You couldn't be in a room with them and not feel it," she said quietly.

It was too much. I let my head fall against the pillow. I needed sleep.

When I woke up the next morning, the first thing I saw was a postcard propped up on my night-stand. I recognized my dad's style immediately. It was a picture of a woman wearing a long red dress. Her chin was raised, defiant almost, but smiling, and her happiness shone through like the sun. It was my mom.

15

The stiffness in my hand brought it all back. It was still early enough to make it to school, but I didn't know if I had the energy. I felt like Gulliver — strapped to the ground by thousands of Lilliputian ropes. So I just lay there. I could hear the house's regular morning noises: Joni calling for Mad to get out of the bathroom, Beth blending something in the kitchen, Mom grinding the beans for her coffee. Maybe if I just stayed here, they'd all leave, and I could spend the day watching television and pretending that my life didn't actually suck.

But then Mom poked her head in the door. For some reason I grabbed the postcard and pulled it under the covers. I don't think she noticed.

"Don't even think about staying home today, Ben."

"I was just getting up."

She stood there in her teacher's clothes looking very put together, but it was a costume. She was as unsure as anybody, when it came right down to it.

Gayle Friesen

And right now there was a canyon of uncertainty hollowed out between us.

Then Beth called her to the phone. She picked up in the hall. "I've got it," she called out.

Through the open doorway I could hear her end of the conversation. I strained to hear, wondering if it was Mrs. Belado with news. Maybe Stan had come home.

"Oh, Jim ... hi ... yes, fine," she said. (I wondered what it would take before she'd say, To tell you the truth things are pretty rotten.) She just chatted amiably, and then her voice changed. "Oh no, I couldn't. I have my aunt visiting and, well, I'm so busy studying, but thanks for asking."

Had this guy asked her out on a date? At eight in the morning? From the sudden chill in her voice, I'd put money on it. This was too weird. She hadn't dated anyone, ever. It never even entered my mind that she might want to. Maybe if she'd seemed interested, it would have occurred to me but ...

She put the phone down, and I thought I heard a sigh. Regret? Or just tiredness.

As I walked to the bathroom, she was still standing by the phone.

"Who was that?"

She looked surprised to see me. "How's your hand?" She sounded concerned.

"Fine. Who was on the phone?"

She looked at the telephone like it might have the answer on it. "Oh, that — just someone from

178

school. It was nothing. I need to get going, Ben, but we'll talk some more after school, okay?"

I grunted and closed the bathroom door behind me. If she didn't want to talk about her life, why should I tell her about mine?

～　～　～

At breakfast, Aunt Frieda said that she needed to start thinking about going home. She said she didn't want to overstay her welcome. It jarred me to think of her leaving — which was funny since I hadn't really wanted her to come. But now her leaving would add another hole to our already punctured house.

"But you still need to show me how to make *zwiebach*," said Beth.

"And *platz*," added Mad.

"And those funny-looking peppermint cookies," chimed Joni.

"*Pfeffermente kuchen*."

Joni tried out the word, and Aunt Frieda laughed.

"She's teaching me *pladeutsch*," Joni told me, breaking her vow of silence.

I kept eating my cereal. They'd all become so cozy. Aunt Frieda'd been accepted into the club. She and I had spent all the time together in the beginning. But now she was one of them. My chest tightened, and I couldn't get any more food down. I pushed my bowl away.

"I can stay a few more days, but then I really must get going," Aunt Frieda insisted.

They offered more reasons why she should stay, but eventually they left and the house was quiet.

"I should get going too." But I made no move to get up. "Why did you leave that picture beside my bed?" I heard myself ask.

"I wanted you to know how your father saw your mother."

"Well, I figured he must have loved her. I mean, she can hardly say his name without getting all choked up."

Her eyes grew sad. "Sometimes I think that type of love — it's especially hard on the children."

I wasn't even going to pretend that I understood. "I really have to go — I'm going to be late."

～   ～   ～

School was a blur of T-shirts and backpacks and noise. I kept watching faces as I went from class to class. Who knew what anyone was really thinking at any given time. I saw Melody with her friends and they looked happy, but then they always did. Was it possible that they were always happy? Max Ton's face flew by with that look of intense concentration, like maybe there was something more he should be doing — some other book he could be reading if only he didn't have to waste precious minutes transporting himself from place to place. Kat caught my eye across the cafeteria, gave me a sweet smile, but it just made me sad about what would never be.

Mostly I was feeling dead inside. And I could see how a person might want to stay that way.

I couldn't face history, and I knew I was guaranteeing myself a failing grade by skipping yet another class; but I did it anyway. I went to the park instead … sat there on a bench like a homeless person until it started to rain.

——— ——— ———

Beth created a feast of borscht and buns for supper. "Mennonite Night" she called it, in honor of Aunt Frieda's many cooking classes.

Aunt Frieda pronounced the meal to be as good as all the ancestors combined could have created, and Beth beamed. Mad prattled on about her commercial, and even Joni seemed happy, eating farmer sausage without preaching on the evils of animal fat. Mom kept glancing over at me, but I mostly kept my head down, dunking the still-warm buns in the broth.

After dinner, Mom asked me into the living room.

She started right in. "I spoke with your history teacher today, Ben."

Shepherd. I froze. Had he told her about the day of the fight? The details?

"He thinks he knows who beat you up, although he didn't feel he could divulge that information to me. Is that what this fight at the gym and the rock throwing was about? Are you afraid of this boy?"

My mother, Sherlock Holmes. Finally asking some questions. But I didn't have any answers for her.

"You told me you didn't see who hurt you. I assumed you were telling the truth. Now I don't know what to believe, Ben. Help me understand." Her eyes were pleading, but they didn't move me. I kept thinking about what Aunt Frieda had said. About how much my mom and dad loved each other. About how hard it was on the kids. Maybe Mom had never loved me, maybe she couldn't. Maybe she had no love left. So I just felt confused. Like I didn't know what she wanted from me.

"Ben, say something." It was an order.

Maybe she was just ticked off that I hadn't told her the truth ... a technicality. I felt bad and I didn't. Being quiet was the only thing I could do, so at least it was honest. Maybe I even wanted her to be angry — yell and scream at me, show something. Instead she left.

Later that night I went to Aunt Frieda's bedroom. She was sitting at the window with her big black book open across her knees. "Come in, Ben. I was just thinking about you."

I sat down on her bed. I wondered what this room would be like when she left. Somehow she'd managed to put her mark on it without changing a thing. Even Joni's picture looked less scary with the old lady here.

"I haven't told you yet when my nightmares ended?"

I smiled. Another bedtime story.

"Let me see, I told you about my dream, that I was in the prison with the guard?"

I nodded, looking into her deeply lined face ... aged by her stories. I thought I could see my father's features in her face, the same image I'd seen at the gym the day I'd fought Alec. And I could hear my old dance teacher's voice. "The most useful images are drawn from your most familiar memories." But my father's face wasn't a familiar memory. I could hardly remember anything about him.

"Ben?"

"Oh, uh, I'm listening."

"After that dream about the guard, I stopped having the nightmares about the lice. I was still alone and still waiting, but the hatred and rage — they were gone."

"But, Aunt Frieda, you still have those nightmares. Here in this house you've had them. Maybe a person can never forget that kind of thing ... or the hatred." The words spilled out of my mouth.

"Oh, Ben. One never forgets, of course not. The events of a person's life become a part of who they are. It would be like forgetting the sound of your beating heart."

"Then what's the point?" I blurted out, and I could hear Alec saying, "You've missed the point."

She sighed. "I've had a good life, Ben. Even with all the horror — or maybe because of it — I've learned what joy is. The years I had with Henry in Canada after he was released, finding my brother Benjamin and his family again. My son. Meeting Jacob's bride. I've had years and years of happiness."

"Then why do you still have the nightmares?"

"The impatience of youth," she smiled. "*Mein bengel*, you want everything to make sense right now. But how could I lie to you and say that everything is good and fine when we both know life is not that simple?

"When I came here to your home and found a scattered place — lives wandering in so many different directions — I went back to a time in my life when I also wandered. My dreams remembered. I think I was dreaming them for you."

"But how, why? You didn't even know me."

"We're family. I felt you needed to hear my story, and I needed to know yours. I know you've sat beside my bed when I've had my nightmares."

And we both knew she'd sat beside mine.

"Hatred is like a fire, Ben. It warms you at first, but eventually it burns more and more of you — your very soul. For years I fostered that kind of hatred. It filled every part of me — but at such high cost."

"Why? What did it cost?"

Aunt Frieda stroked the book on her lap in silence.

"It cost me my son," she said softly. "I thank God now that he left when he did with the Rempel family. They were able to raise him with the love I had no room for. A heart can only hold so much."

"You were glad your son was gone?" I looked at her, shocked. She was sticking a knife between my ribs. Maybe it was me personally she was talking about.

"Of course not." She shook her head sadly. "It broke my heart."

"Then how ... what ..." I struggled for words.

"A heart full of hatred is numb. But a broken heart is felt right to the quick. And a broken heart can be mended."

"How?"

"I remembered the faith of my people. A faith that could only fill an empty vessel. And by then, *mein bengel*, I was empty."

"I don't get it," I said. "I'm sorry, I just don't."

"You will, Ben. Remember when you taught me to dance?"

"Yeah."

"You told me to find the music? You weren't talking about notes and melodies, were you?"

"Not exactly."

"You were talking about the rhythm that beats deep inside you ... the rhythm that guides your steps, yes?"

It seemed so long ago that I'd said those words. When was the last time I'd felt anything was guiding me?

"Do you ever feel really, really old, Aunt Frieda?" I asked, but as soon as the words were out, I could hear how stupid they sounded.

"I have never felt as old as I did when the hatred ruled my life. These wrinkles are just a disguise." She smiled broadly. "Some days now, when I watch a beautiful sunrise — or the day I danced — I feel as if I've just been born."

I watched her eyes, clear and sparkling and still young.

Joni walked into the room then, and I just about fell off my chair. She was dressed in a bright blue sweater. I hadn't seen her in anything but black for as long as I could remember.

"Can you sit for me now, Aunt Frieda?"

Aunt Frieda squeezed my hand as she stood. "Joni's painting my portrait. I'm going to be famous — like Whistler's mother!" She grinned.

"You're painting actual people now, Joni?" I asked, surprised.

"Only actual people."

16

"Ben, telephone!" Mom called down the stairs.

It was Stan's mom. He was in the youth detention center. He'd busted a guy's jaw. For some weird
reason, Stan's mom told me it was wired shut. I
hung up the phone in a daze.

Stan was back.

～ ～ ～

Fish met me at my locker the next day after lunch.

"She called you, too?" he said.

"Yeah. Last night."

"He's back."

"I guess."

I don't know why, but Fish looked like a stranger
to me. Everything looked strange.

"Do you know where this place is?" I asked.

"Downtown," he answered vaguely.

"I'm going to visit him tonight. You coming?"

"I don't know, man. I've got this thing with
Melody."

"A thing?"

"I don't know."

"Forget it. I'll tell him you said hi." I slammed my locker door and walked down the hall. Big, strong Fish couldn't handle it. I left the school then. I already knew more than I wanted to know.

Claude and company caught up with me half-way home. Apart from an occasional sighting at school, I hadn't seen him since the day he sent me to the hospital.

"Hey, Ballerina Boy, got any steps you want to teach me?"

Echoed laughs from behind encouraged him and he smirked.

"Just say when and where, jerk," I growled back.

"Ooh, tough guy. Your slippers too tight?" he said, but seemed surprised.

"Yeah, that's it." I leaned toward him. My heart was booming. My fists were ready.

He looked around to make sure his friends were still there. "Dance this Friday. Eight o'clock, behind the gym."

"I'll be there." I left them howling with empty, stupid laughter.

━━ ━━ ━━

There was no soup bubbling on the stove, no smells of cooking meat, no *zwiebach*, golden brown on the cooling racks. No signs of life. Mom had said something about going to the travel agency with Aunt Frieda to arrange for her trip home. And our trip back to — what had she called it? — a place of scattered lives?

I put my head down on the kitchen table. I could hear the clock in the hallway. I'd never really heard it before, never been aware of such silence that I'd welcome a ticking clock. I must have fallen asleep, because the next thing I knew there was a crick like a boomerang in my neck. I stretched and looked at my watch. It was already three o'clock. If I didn't want Mom asking questions about why I was home so early, I needed to leave, now. I grabbed a couple of cookies and looked up the address of the detention center. Two buses at least.

It took me an hour to get to the formidable gates. Detention center, nothing. This was a prison. I beeped the intercom, gave my name and a faceless person buzzed me in. I was taken to a cold room filled with metal tables and chairs. Parents or social workers sat across from their kids with angry, worried, nervous expressions. A dozen stories. I sat down and felt a shiver all over. The hall echoed with hushed voices — the odd shrill word being quieted immediately.

The door opened, and Stan walked in. He looked older — decades older — and thinner. But tougher, too. Sinewy, Joni would have said. He had a shadowy face now, and in this fluorescent light, the stubble looked like evidence of every day he'd been gone.

I half stood, but the guard or whatever he was glared me back down.

"Stan."

There was no smile, of course, almost no look of recognition from him.

"I bought you some books on the way here," I blurted stupidly, not knowing what else to say.

He looked down before sitting. He only touched the books to push them back across the chipped tabletop. This was a bad sign.

"Conrad. Good of you to come, old boy," he said, and I felt an enormous relief at the sound of his voice, even if it was husky and shadowy like his face. "Did you bring any smokes?"

"Geez, I didn't think of it. Sorry. Next time."

He lifted one hand lazily. "No matter."

"Where've you been, Stan? What have you done?"

"It was the best of times, it was the worst of times," he said, quoting again. "No, just the worst of times."

"What happened? Some guy, your mom said — a broken jaw? Did somebody jump you?"

He looked at me then, and what I saw sent the chill of death right through me. Stone, flat and hard, where his eyes should have been.

"You still dancing, young Ben?"

Was he making fun of me? Him too?

"What?"

"Didn't you give up, too? Isn't that what this whole stinking life is about? Hanging on for as long as you can and then just giving up. Huh, young Ben? Isn't that what it's about?" His voice rose above the acceptable level, and our guard moved a step closer.

Stan put his finger to his lips in an exaggerated whisper. "Shh, we have to behave or else they might put us in jail. Oops." He clapped both hands over his mouth. "Too late. We're already here."

"One more outburst and your visitor will have to leave." The anonymous gray person found a voice.

"And that would be such a shame," Stan said softly. "My first guest, and all."

The gray guy backed off a step.

"Your parents haven't been here?"

"It would cause my mother too much pain to see me in such a place, so she said. Now my father, he did show up — to tell me what a disappointment I was, hardly a guest appearance."

Stan was breathing heavily, but nothing else about him moved.

"I should've brought some smokes, Stan. I'm sorry."

"Don't be sorry, Ben." His eyes melted a little then, just a little. "There's nothing you could have done. It was coming for a long time."

"What was coming?"

Nothing.

"Stan. What was coming?"

"A big old bus, Ben. And I couldn't get out of the way." His eyes wandered above my head.

"What are you talking about?"

"I tried to move, get out of the way — how is he?" His eyes looked panicked.

"Who?"

"The guy ..."

The guy with the wired jaw. "He'll be fine, Stan. Tell me why."

At first I didn't think he was going to say anything. He just sat there. But I waited.

"I was in a phone booth, trying to work up the guts to call home. I just wanted to go home, Ben. But this guy kept yammering at me to get off the phone and I ... I lost it. I couldn't stop hitting him. I was just so ... angry ... at him, at ... everybody." Stan's hands were shaking even as he drummed them relentlessly on the table. "I just lost it ..."

"We all make mistakes, Stan." I sounded small and trite.

"You wouldn't understand, Ben. You're a good guy, you're okay."

"You'll be okay."

His eyes told me that he didn't believe me. But before I could say anything else, the gray guy took him away, saying our time was up.

When they finally told me to leave, I picked up the books I'd bought — some Russian guy whose name I couldn't pronounce. I asked the man at the front desk to give them to Stan.

～～ ～～ ～～

The first bus dropped me off close to the church where Aunt Frieda had gone. As I walked past it to the next bus stop, I hesitated. Then I crossed the street.

Before I knew it, I was at the front doors and pulling. Wrong. The doors were locked. I kicked them with such force that they shook at the hinges. What happened to churches being open all night for weary passersby, like in the movies? It wasn't even that late.

A man in a jean jacket and a buzz cut poked his head around the corner of the building. He was carrying a computer case. "Can I help you?" he asked.

"I, uh, I'm sorry. I just wanted — never mind." I went down the stairs two at a time and tried to walk past without meeting his eyes.

"No need to be sorry. It's a tough old building. What did you want?"

"Nothing. I'm sorry."

"You know, I might have left my sermon notes inside. If you want to go in for a bit, that's fine."

He had already taken his keys out and was climbing the stairs to open the door. I knew he was lying about forgetting something, and I was so surprised that a man of the cloth (even in a jean jacket) would tell a fib, I followed him.

I didn't know what to do when I got inside. I think I was expecting a big huge space with burning candles and stained-glass windows. I was expecting altars. Maybe choir boys. Maybe I needed to stop watching so much television.

But burgundy carpeting and a coffeepot in the lobby and evenly spaced padded benches were definitely a surprise.

"I'll just be in the back for a bit. Let me know if you need anything?" He looked expectant.

"Ben."

"I'm Matt," he said, stretching out his hand. I shook it.

"Do you guys give, um, advice or anything?"

He smiled. "Now and then. Not that anybody listens." He undid his jacket and sat down. "How can I help you?"

He was pretty young, this guy. By Aunt Frieda's standards anyway. Early forties. Probably the guy she had talked about.

"My aunt comes here once in a while. She likes it." I checked out the instruments and amplifiers on the stage. "Except for the drums. She could do without the drums."

"I've heard that before," he said. "You should

have heard the complaints when we went from green to blue hymnals."

"Oh no, I mean, she was cool with it. She's pretty cool."

"What's her name? I wonder if I've met her."

"Frieda. Her name's Frieda."

"Just Frieda? Like Cher?"

I laughed. "Um, not quite." I couldn't think of her last name. Actually, I'd never thought of her as having a last name. "But she's going home soon."

"Sounds like you'll miss her."

"Yeah, I guess. But that's not why — you know, I should get going."

"Okay, but you look like you've got something on your mind."

"Kinda. It's just that, well, my friend is in trouble."

"Your friend?" he asked kindly.

It took me a minute. "Yeah, no really, my friend, Stan. I guess people say that all the time though, huh? It's their friend, but really it's them? But, honest to … well, honest." I was babbling — and lying. "Okay, me then." That was a relief. Besides, he wasn't going to tell anyone. It was like that priest thing. Client confidentiality.

"Listen, you probably want to get home, right?" I got up to leave.

"Not really." He waved me down. "I just spent an hour on the phone discussing whether we should serve farmer sausage or hot dogs at the next potluck. Believe me, I welcome something juicier."

I must have looked confused.

"Sorry, Ben. I'm not making light of your problem. Go ahead."

"No offense, but do you have a clue how things are, you know, out there?"

"Why don't you tell me," he said quietly.

I took a deep breath. "Mostly it's this guy, this jerk whose mission in life is to separate my nose from my face."

"And his reason?"

"Besides being a creep?"

"Besides that."

I was twitchy. I didn't really want to get into this. What could he do anyhow?

"You know, maybe this was a bad idea."

"Okay, Ben. You've got this kid at school who wants to hurt you. Maybe he's already hurt you?"

I nodded.

"I could tell you that you should inform the authorities." I started to object, but he kept talking. "But you know that. I do know how dangerous it is out there. God didn't exactly plan my nose this way," he said, pointing to a bump on the bridge.

"A fight?"

"Well, kind of. Smashed into a door running away from a fight, actually. There were four guys — and one of me."

I couldn't help smiling. He laughed. "Nobody ever accused me of being the bravest kid on the block."

"But you can't always run away."

He shook his head. "No. But running isn't the only option. There are others. Do you know much about pacifism, Ben?"

I shrugged. "Like Gandhi?"

He nodded. "Well, the Mennonites have always — "

"Mennonites?" I interrupted. I almost laughed.

"What?" He looked surprised. "This *is* a Mennonite church. You've heard of them?"

"There's a lot of it going around lately."

He looked puzzled but continued. "Well, it's fairly complicated, in a way. And you'll get all sorts of definitions. But to me, pacifism means not running away from yourself."

"Come again?"

"Think about it. In every society at every point in history there have been wars. It's always been that way, probably always will be. People fight — over land, over religion … over a girl. And it's not who's right — if anyone. It's usually about strength. Strong guy, army, country rolls over the weak."

"I guess."

"That's why it never ends. There's always somebody a little stronger. Refusing to fight means that you're saying the fighting ends here. Strength is not truth." He stopped, scratched his head. "I did eventually fight that kid, one on one. We both ended up with black eyes, but he was the one on the floor."

"So, did he ever bug you again?"

"No, he didn't. But I'd grown a foot that summer. He started picking on smaller kids. The point is, Ben, I lost something that day."

"What did you lose? You won the fight. Maybe the point is you got the guy off your back."

"And onto someone else's. But I still hated the guy. And an enemy like that has a lot of power over you."

I thought of all my days and nights of rage, my nightmares about Claude. "Maybe."

"I think when you stop hating, you set yourself free."

"But the other guy goes free, too."

He thought awhile, tapped a book in front of him. "True, Ben, but you get to live your life bigger."

I sat staring in front of me, thinking about that.

"I hope you'll come back sometime, Ben. And I hope things work out for you."

He walked me to the doors then, ushered me through and locked up.

I said good-bye and ran to catch the bus that was pulling up to the stop. And I almost got on, but then I didn't. I walked over to the park instead. Buses made me think of Stan, how he'd said he couldn't get out of the way. But maybe he could have. I had to believe that.

As I ran around the track, Matt's words pounded in my head. They sounded really good in a safe, warm building. But out here? I thought of Aunt Frieda hiding in the orchard knowing that God was listening to the songs of a thousand languages. But could he hear mine?

17

Aunt Frieda was going to leave on Saturday morning, and I felt bad about missing her last night with us, but she insisted I go to the dance. She said it was important for me to go. It almost seemed she knew.

She cooked all of our favorite foods for supper, but they stuck in my throat.

As I dressed for the dance, I was nervous but not scared. I wasn't thinking I was going to get whipped. I knew better. I was going to crush Claude.

"I'm glad you're getting out," Mom said. She'd been pretty decent to me since Stan came back. I figured she felt sorry for me. Or maybe she was scared that I was going to end up sharing his cell.

As I was about to leave, I caught Aunt Frieda's eye. She smiled and then came over and gave me a hug. In my ear, or as close as she could come to it, she whispered, "Just find the music."

I looked down at her, tried to smile but couldn't.

As I walked to the school, I concentrated on mustering up the blood lust I'd felt when I'd fought with Alec, my rage when I saw that torn crinoline in the nurse's office.

——— ——— ———

The gym was decorated with balloons and streamers, and the music was cheesy retro disco, of all things. I scanned the crowd for Claude. There was no sign of him. Briefly I hoped that he wouldn't show up. It would solve everything if he didn't.

Kat was there. I saw her immediately. She was wearing a white dress, off her shoulders, a peasant kind of thing. She made me think of Aunt Frieda's Russian couple and their music. No. I pushed my hands tightly together, enough to feel pain. I wouldn't think about that now. Only Claude. And Claude's goons holding my arms while he tore up my face, split my lip, ripped up my shoulder. Claude's eyes ... that's what I needed to focus on. He was the bad guy.

"You're a good guy, Ben," Stan had said. Stan, who'd shattered a guy's jaw so that it had to be held together with wire. What did that make him?

My body started shaking. I looked for somewhere to go until it stopped. What if I beat Claude to a pulp? What did that make me? I pushed my way through the crowd.

"Why do there have to be bad guys? Makes it easier to shoot them ..."

By the time I reached the edge of the gym, I was soaked with sweat. A hand reached out and grabbed my shoulder. I spun, ready to fight.

"Hey!" Kat moved back. "I just wanted to know if you, well, felt like dancing? I hear you're pretty good."

I looked at her beautiful face and everything started to spin.

"Are you okay, Ben? Do you need some water? Are you drunk?"

I couldn't answer. I was so far from okay I couldn't even see it.

"I thought I told you to stay away from certain girls," Claude said, walking up to us. "You look nice, Kat. How about a dance?" He leaned on her shoulder.

"I'd rather eat dirt," she said, pushing him away.

"Don't tell me you're interested in Ballerina Boy?" he said, grabbing her waist. He swayed, having obviously downed a few pints before the dance. "Hey," he said to me over his shoulder. "It's a dance, and you didn't wear your tutu."

That did it. "Let's go. Outside."

"Don't give me orders," he hissed.

Suddenly there was a space around us as people moved back to give us room. The music was blaring. I could hear it, feel it, "*Oo, oo, oo, oo, stayin' alive, stayin' alive.*"

"Wanna dance?" I sneered, moving around him in our makeshift ring, roped in by curious spectators. Somebody laughed, which infuriated Claude.

He swiped at me, missing. He was bigger but clumsier. He didn't stand a chance. He was mine. I ducked easily under a second attempt and bobbed up behind him, the back of his head well within striking distance. Badly choreographed, Miss Fleur would have said — I wouldn't hit him in the back.

"Over here," I called.

He roared and charged me. For a second we wrestled — an ugly *pas de deux* — and then we hit the floor. I twisted and rolled and stood again while he struggled to regain his balance. He was half sitting and an easy target — but I wouldn't hit a sitting duck.

I waved. "Song's almost over, big guy. Get on your feet."

He should have taken time to regain his balance, and he stumbled. He was so close. But I just kept moving around. Floating. Claude was snorting like a bull by this time.

"Hit him," one of his goons stage-whispered to him.

Claude turned on his friend. "You hit him!"

Claude looked at me then. He could see me. But I couldn't see anything beyond his dark, dilated pupils. It was as though they had absorbed all the light around us. I knew it then. He needed to fight me. But I didn't need to fight him. If I did, I'd become him.

It would have been easy to avoid the blow I saw coming, and I couldn't really say why I didn't, except that I wanted to see this thing finished, to move through the pain, the way Alec was always saying. Or maybe I saw Stan in his eyes. All I knew was that I wasn't going to let hatred define me. So I stood there. As the blow connected with my cheek, I felt the pressure and the pain, but I held my ground, my arms hanging loosely at my sides.

Claude stared at me. The crowd grew quiet, letting the music into our ring. *"Stayin' alive, stayin' alive."*

"What's wrong with you? Fight me." He was almost pleading.

I shook my head, and ever so slightly I turned my face toward him. I didn't take my eyes off his. I wanted him to see me when he hit me again. I wanted him to know who I was.

But the blow didn't come. Claude just muttered something like "He's crazy," and he stomped out of the gym with his confused buddies in tow.

As he retreated, people clapped. That's when I noticed that Fish was there, smiling — and Shepherd. He could've stopped the fight, maybe he should have. But he hadn't. He gave a little nod, then disappeared back to the chaperon shadows.

I smiled, embarrassed at the commotion. I thought I could hear Aunt Frieda saying, "Just find the music." I closed my eyes. And there it was. And I said, "Thank you."

"Huh?"

A voice brought me back to the present. I opened my eyes.

"What did you say?" Kat asked.

"I, uh, said, do you want to dance? I hear I'm pretty good."

"Pretty conceited," she said, smiling back.

I took her by the elbow and led her to the center of the floor. I could feel my cheek swell with the bruise that I'd have tomorrow, but I didn't mind, because I was feeling again.

And we danced.

I walked Kat home and sort of lost track of time after that. At home I stopped by Aunt Frieda's room, but it was silent inside. I listened for sounds of nightmares, but there were none.

That night I had a dream that was as clear as a painting. I was five years old, about to start kindergarten. I was walking down the street holding someone's hand. It was a big hand, big and warm. I was asking all sorts of questions — what was I going to learn? Would the teacher be nice? What if I had to go to the bathroom, would she let me go? I was really concerned about that one.

"Of course," the man said. "Of course she'll let you go."

Even in my dream state, a shiver ran up my spine. I recognized the voice. It was the voice that had read bedtime stories to me. I could feel the bigness of his hand, hear the low, soothing bass of his voice. I could even smell the paint thinner. It was as though all my senses were remembering what I'd never forgotten.

As I came out of the schoolyard, I saw my dream self through the eyes of the man who waited for me.

That's when I woke up. I rushed upstairs. On the landing I pulled at the attic cord and yanked. Stairs came down with a groan from lack of use. I headed straight to the corner of the room, to the paintings covered with a sheet. I rummaged through until I found it. Then I leaned back and stared.

It was my elementary school, and children were coming out of the side entrance. A little kid was looking at the artist. His face was full of wonder and excitement and news. It was me. Looking at my dad.

Tears burned in my eyes. Then I heard something behind me.

"Ben?"

My mom was standing at the top of the stairs wrapped in her ratty blue bathrobe. She still looked half-asleep.

I wiped the tears away. "Yeah, I'm ... did Dad take me to kindergarten that first day?"

"Did Dad take ... well, yes, I think. Yes, of course he did."

"So he did? He walked with me?"

Mom sat down on a crate and rubbed her eyes. "Neil wanted to be the one to ... How did you know this, Ben? I don't remember telling you."

"You didn't. I had a dream, and then I remembered this painting. In my dream it felt really good ... safe."

She nodded. "He was excited about taking you, Ben. And he wanted to be the first face you'd see waiting outside the school."

"He was, see?" I pointed to the painting.

"He rushed up here as soon as he came home," she said, smiling. "He wanted to capture the moment." Her eyes drifted away from mine. "He was always so good at that." Her voice grew wistful.

It was as if I could actually see her begin to disappear, one particle at a time.

"We're still here, Mom."

"Your father was an amazing man, Ben. He turned my life upside down and inside out — until I was dizzy." She sat back, leaning against an unfinished wall, pink insulation all around her.

"You see, when I was growing up ... my parents loved me but everything was about being proper and cool — never raise your voice, don't show too much of, well, anything." She smiled sadly. "Your dad would say, 'If you feel it — say it, shout it.'" Her hand reached out to stroke a canvas. "Paint it. I married him, loving him with all my heart and against all good judgment. I knew he'd take me places I'd never go on my own — and I trusted him. And then he died." Her voice was a whisper now and I had to strain to hear. "He was supposed to help, Ben. He was supposed to provide ... the color." She looked so sad then, so lost, and I didn't have a clue how to reach her.

Then she got to her feet. "But I want you to give me some credit, Ben. Not thanks, just credit. I have worked my ass off the past ten years for this family. I've gotten up every single morning. I've gone to work, and studied, and tried to make something better for us. And I think I've done a good job of that." Her chin was raised, and her words were a challenge.

"I agree."

Some of the wind seemed to go out of her when I said that.

"You do?"

"Yeah, I do. Now I do."

"Oh."

"Don't move," I said, and ran downstairs to my room. I reached inside the drawer of my nightstand. Then I raced upstairs again.

I was breathing heavily by the time I got there, and I handed her the postcard Dad had done of her.

I pointed at the woman in the picture. Chin raised, arms crossed. Eyes shining with defiance and humor, love and light. "I can see that person."

Her eyes filled with tears. "You can?"

I nodded. "Yeah, when you yell about working your ass off. I can totally see ... what he saw."

She ran her hands through her hair. "Oh, Ben." She shook her head, closing her eyes. "Last night Aunt Frieda told me about her time in Russia."

I nodded.

"I never understood it before. I never realized how much she'd lost — what a survivor she is. When your father died, I just accepted that part of me died with him and the rest has been going through the motions. I haven't really been living."

"I know."

"You and Joni both. You know me the best, I think. Maybe it's because you're so much like your father." She reached out and touched the back of my hand. "She told me something else last night, Ben."

I waited.

"She told me not to lose you."

I thought about my dream, and how my father had held my hand. It was so big, almost wrapping around mine. Now Mom's small hand was wrapped in mine.

"Somewhere along the way you've become a man, Ben. I don't want to lose you, too."

Then she leaned over and hugged me. "I love you," she said. And it was sufficient.

She pulled away and sniffed loudly, wiping away her tears. "So," she said in her old, matter-of-fact voice — it kind of startled me. "The thing is, there's this guy ... from work."

"Jim?" I guessed, remembering the phone conversation.

"Jim," she said. "Anyway, he's asked me to this dance and, of course, I'm a terrible dancer. But maybe, I wonder, could you ... I mean, if you can have an eighty-five-year-old woman sashaying around the living room, maybe there's some hope for me."

"Maybe. But don't forget Aunt Frieda's a natural."

And I hugged her.

18

After I showered, I went to call Aunt Frieda to breakfast. Mom was going to take her to the airport after we'd eaten the waffles she had made. My mom, actually cooking. I figured maybe it was some sort of statement.

I knocked at the door, softly at first, then more insistently.

"Come in."

Aunt Frieda sat in the chair by the window. The sunlight streamed in, bathing the room in morning gold. She was dressed in a blue suit: skirt, blouse and jacket, ready for her trip home.

I had meant to say, Breakfast's ready, but what came out was "Do you have to go?"

"You know what they say about houseguests and fish going bad after three days," she smiled. "And I've been here much longer."

I sat down on the bed. "You know when you came, like at first? I didn't know if you'd, well, fit in. But now I can't imagine this room … us … without you."

"Oh, things will return to normal soon enough."

"I hope not."

"My mother used to sew quilts, Ben — beautiful quilts pieced together with odd bits of clothing that we'd all worn at one time or another. It was a wonder the threads even held together after our brood was through wearing them. But somehow she'd salvage bits and pieces and bring them together as something new. Still, every patch, every square held a memory, a story — a bruised knee, a church social, a Christmas dress. When I look at your family, Ben, that's what I see — a beautiful quilt still in the making. It's taken me a lifetime to follow the threads of my life. This time with your family has been very special to me. It's reminded me that I have a place in the world, a reason for being."

She sat straighter and sniffed the air. "*Nah yo.* I smell something delicious."

"Mom's making waffles."

"Your mother is cooking?"

She sounded so surprised that I laughed out loud. "See what you started?"

The mood was somewhat somber in the kitchen. But the reviews of the waffles were positive.

"Very good, Mom," Beth announced after two very thoughtful bites.

Mom grinned. "They are, aren't they? I hope I've made enough." It was weird, but nice to hear her sounding so much like a mom. I knew the cooking wouldn't last — Beth would face a firing squad before surrendering her kitchen. Still, it was nice to see Mom so ... here.

Suddenly I was starving. I grabbed three waffles — and the girls hollered.

"It's okay," Mom intervened. "He's a growing boy."

"That's right," I said with my mouth full.

"Just try to keep your mouth closed — maybe till you've grown," Joni grumbled.

"They're very tasty, Catherine," Aunt Frieda said.

"Thank you, Frieda," Mom answered softly.

After Joni had finished her breakfast, she took her plate to the sink and left the room without a word.

She returned hugging a canvas to her. You couldn't see what was on it because she held it so tightly against her sweater, and her face was pale pink.

Then she handed the picture to Aunt Frieda. "I want you to have it."

Aunt Frieda held the picture out at arm's length and studied it. Even from where I was sitting I could tell it was good. But when she held it up. I knew it was more than just good, it was beautiful. The grays and blacks were still there, but Joni had added light. You could see a picture emerging from the shadows. Or maybe it was the light emerging — I couldn't tell. But it was clearly Aunt Frieda in the forefront. Some of the lines in her face appeared softened by Joni's brush, but when I looked closer, I realized that the lines were still there — it was the radiance in her eyes that outshone everything else.

In the background was another distinct figure, farther away, less defined — our dad. And around him stood clusters of people, lines and curves mostly, but definitely people. Aunt Frieda's brothers and sisters? Our great-aunts and uncles? Strangers, but now part of us.

Finally Aunt Frieda broke the silence. "It's lovely, Joni." She had tears sparkling in her eyes. She passed her hand over the figures, not touching, only skimming the surface of the painting. "But it's so precious. You should keep it here with you."

Joni shook her head. "I want you to have it. Really. Besides, the den could use a new mural, a new look. Time for a change."

Aunt Frieda nodded. "Yes, it is."

"I think we should propose a toast," I said, surprising myself.

"Good idea," Mad said, starting to stand.

Joni frowned her down. "Let him do it."

Amazingly Mad obeyed.

I stood, holding my orange juice. I felt awkward and was tempted to sit down again, but I wanted to do this, and I wanted to do it right. I coughed to loosen my vocal cords.

"Well, I'd just like to say, um, first of all ..." I looked around and almost lost my nerve, but Aunt Frieda's bird-like posture, head thrust forward, made me smile. "Well, you're really old."

The girls laughed and Mom said, "Ben," with only mild disapproval. Aunt Frieda nodded with a glint in her eyes.

"And you're very smart and kind of pushy. You tell great stories and I think ..." I looked into her eyes. "I think maybe you stitched us together."

"To Aunt Frieda," we said.

～　　～　　～

After her bags had been checked, we hovered around Aunt Frieda just outside the security gate. She looked up at us, tears flooding the rims of her soft brown eyes.

"I love you all," she said simply.

She hugged the girls one by one, lingering with my mother, who, it seemed, held on the longest.

Finally she turned to me. "*Nah yo, mein bengel.*"

"You ... helped me," I said, my voice cracking a little. I reached down and hugged her.

"We helped each other."

Then she straightened to her full height, such as it was, and her many years were apparent on that face that had lived forever.

"You take care of each other," she said, and then she was gone.

～　　～　　～

When we got back home, I told Mom I was going for a walk.

"Anywhere in particular?" Mad asked, eyes twinkling.

"Leave him be," Mom ordered, and I smiled my appreciation.

I followed my tracks from the night before. My heart pounded a rhythm that I fell into until I was almost jogging.

As I approached her house, I made myself slow down. "Cool it, Conrad," I muttered.

But I wasn't feeling cool. I couldn't keep the grin off my face.

I saw her before she saw me. She was in the driveway practicing her jump shots. She was so good. She was so pretty.

Then the old nervousness appeared, and the voice that told me that she was way, way out of my league. Last night's dance had never happened ... it was a dream. I was dreaming to think she'd be interested in me.

I could turn around and she'd never know. Ducking behind a tree, I took a deep breath. The blossoms obscured my view, and I knew how stupid it must look — a kid hiding under a cherry tree. I pushed a branch out of my way to get a better view. Then I thought of Henry. I snapped off a blossom before I could change my mind.

I thought of how it would look in her dark hair and I smiled. I took a step toward the sound of the basketball.

Nah yo.